MIRROR MANIA

MIRROR MANIA

ROVEENA CHAND JASSAL

NEW DEGREE PRESS

MIRROR MANIA

ISBN

978-1-63676-623-2 *Paperback*

978-1-63676-303-3 *Kindle Ebook*

978-1-63676-304-0 *Digital Ebook*

*To those who love me no matter how unbearable
I can be. You know who you are!*

CONTENTS

"An idea is like a virus, resilient, highly contagious, and the smallest seed of an idea can grow to define or destroy you."

—INCEPTION

AUTHOR'S NOTE

When I was eight years old, I distinctly remember having a contest with one of my equally miniature, four-foot-tall friends about who could eat the gooiest S'mores Pop Tarts from my basement pantry. The feeling of being stuffed with dry graham cracker crumbs laden all over my face and admiring how much food she could eat in one sitting left me in awe: the catalyst to my addictive cycle.

After that, I broke a contract with my body and eventually my mind. I stopped listening to her hunger cues and banned her from connecting with my logical mind as well. Everywhere I went, my thoughts revolved around food, specifically on what was the necessary amount I needed to eat just for the sake of staying "skinny" and "desirable." Everywhere I went, I catalogued what and how much I ate. Everywhere I went, my decisions revolved around what I could do to ensure that the number on the scale would decrease. I was parched for control. I was obsessed with maintaining that number.

In high school, I further zombified myself without even realizing it. For three years, I ate absolutely no carbs and I weighed myself up to seven times a day. That was all on the weekdays, of course, but the weekend was my beloved, gluttonous escape, filled with expired triple chocolate muffins and family-sized bags of jalapeño Cheetos. The scale had already taken over my life and my thoughts, ripping apart my soul, body, and mind, exposing vulnerabilities and insecurities that would continue to have their leverage over me. My happiness was the sacrifice I thought I had to make to be "healthy."

"Two pounds over. *You can't go to that party. You don't deserve to go.*"

"*You can't wear that dress. You're not at the right weight to wear that.*"

"*Don't eat with friends. You're strong enough not to. You don't need to.*"

As isolating and personal as this might seem, a surprising number of young people share my challenges with body image and weight. It just isn't talked about enough. In fact, it's not even clearly defined. According to National Eating Disorders Association, negative attitudes toward higher-weight children begin as early as three to five years old. [1]

Although hunger and eating habits are taught to us at this age, we often just *assume* these habits are supposed to be known and innate, so it shouldn't be a struggle. In the developed world, it can be considered a vain issue to have too much to eat and not know what to eat or when to eat, but that is our reality. People naturally look to the media for cues on fashion, makeup trends, where to shop, and, unfortunately, beauty standards as well. We look at different actors, movies, and social accounts. We don't look inside ourselves because we want guidance. We've gotten to this

---

[1]   "Statistics and Research on Eating Disorders," National Eating Disorder Association, accessed on August 5, 2020.

point where weight and the perfect body are now full-time life pursuits:

"Once you're at your goal weight, you can accomplish ANYTHING."

"Only eat from twelve to eight. No carbs. No sugar. Cut out fruits too."

"Lose twenty pounds in two weeks with this new plan!"

Everyone who struggles with body image comes to their struggles in a unique way. I believe my experience originated from being a minority and growing up in a racially diverse community. Judgment was expected if there was extra chub on my face since the last time Dadima (grandmother) came to visit. I've even had guy friends express to me about their own insecurities on how they look, but don't feel safe to talk about them with anyone. Not only do I know what it's like to live life wishing that I could be in a different body or to not go a day without worrying if I'm eating too much, but I also understand the cultural struggles.

All of this pressure and anxiety took up so much of my energy that I didn't have any left to adequately express or deal with my emotions. I lacked mental awareness in how to express myself other than through tearing open bags of Chips Ahoy cookies and slurping tubs of brain-freezing Moose Tracks ice cream down my throat. I didn't know who I was, so I let weight define me. I had spent so much time wishing I looked different that I began wishing I was just a different person overall. My relationships with others were dwindling just as quickly as I lost my relationship with myself. But finally, I had enough.

There have definitely been improvements in accepting different body types or shapes at different weights, but there's still this notion of perfection that media promotes. For instance, many lingerie companies like Aerie, Levi's, and H&M now hire models of all sizes to showcase that beauty comes in many forms. [2]

Recruiters for other careers seem to be relying less on physical appearance for a more objective hiring process, and plus-size clothing is becoming more available in stores as well.

However, we are simultaneously in a similar age of Greek and Roman humanism, working on specific body parts to appear as aesthetically pleasing as possible. Ironically, we seem to eat it up. It's great to have goals and to strive to be healthy, but it's become so overt that if you're not dedicating your entire life to that, then you're viewed as lesser, or dare I say it, *lazy*. More than ever, I believe we have to become aware of how media affects our standards toward life because of how immersed our lives have become in technology.

I believe we need to talk about hunger, sex, emotions, and all the experiences that seem "natural" instead of just assuming that everyone knows how to navigate these aspects of life, because they may not come easily for all of us.

Most importantly, I believe happiness is not determined by numbers or by external factors or conditions, but rather by personal choice. You get to define your reasons for how you live your life. You get to choose what makes you happy.

To fight against the societal pressures that I and so many others feel and hopefully inspire some change, I've written my novel, *Mirror Mania*.

Mirror Mania is a fictional novel for young adults and adults of all genders who struggle with looking at the external, rather than the internal. It's a tale of corporations controlling

---

2   Sophia Westover, "8 Body Positive and Inclusive Sustainable Fashion Brands," *Attire Media*, July 19, 2020.

our lives becoming a reality. I've created a physical manifestation of the horrible thoughts I have faced around my body image and weight in the somewhat futuristic Speculo City, where citizens have tech buttons sewn into their skin connecting them to the mandatory, all-inclusive communication system Facegram. Influencers at Mirror Mania determine every citizen's minimum, maximum, and perfect midpoint body weight. If a citizen goes outside their prescribed numbers, they suffer the consequences that I faced in my anxious mind.

I created this novel to discuss an issue that others usually feel alone in through an entertaining and creative manner. This book encompasses how body image insecurity relates to personal identity and how this shared anxiety is manifested differently for everyone. To further add to the reading experience, I've even added names and places based on real life concepts from Indian, Spanish, Latin, and African influences.

Speculo City is a charming manifestation of how current society is today and what it potentially could entail. Ropashna, an open-hearted and fearless girl over her maximum by twenty pounds refuses to let her weight prevent her from interning at Mirror Mania. Deslin, a cocky and gorgeous twenty-year-old, uses his chiseled exterior to mask his intentions to seek revenge. Together, Ropashna and Deslin have undeniable determination to destroy Mirror Mania once and for all but have no desire to work together. However, the real dilemma is in determining whether destruction will bring true peace to not just the city, but to themselves.

PART 1

BLURRED

CHAPTER 1

HEART AND SOUL: ROPASHNA

———

"Are you deaf?! I already told you that you aren't allowed in here anymore, you fat, ugly bitch! You're thirty pounds over your maximum weight limit. Leave already!" a coarse, harsh voice bleeds into my ears.

I'm the reason that the line to Mirror Mania is backed up, but I don't care. My thick thighs hinge themselves over the greased charcoal gate, pleading to be let in so I can get to Ovatus. Tears fill my eyes and my throat clenches.

"Someone take this fatty away please!"

I start screaming, yelling, and cursing, trying to get someone to see I am on the right side of things. I've always been on the right side.

But my performance is interrupted, and *he* sprints toward me. He's wearing a tight black skinsuit with an embroidered *MM* near his collarbone and leather combat boots. I just can't believe how he could be so heartless after everything. I can't stand my ground any longer. My hair falls in front of my face as I slump into his strong, moon tattooed, veiny arms: a place that once felt so comforting.

And just before the world goes black, I let out a weak laugh.

* * *

Do I regret reaching this point? I sure as hell don't.

This is how it all began: I would eat. All day long.

I would wake up in the morning and get super excited if I was two pounds less than the day before. My sense of confidence revolved around that number. My reward for the week's hard work would be a full-day feast.

"You already ruined your low carb, no sugar diet already, so why stop now?" I would tell myself right after indulging on three small gobs of Chocozaps.

I would then proceed to rip open a family-size Cheezbits bag and start crunching away, ferociously shoving handfuls of Cheezbits in my mouth to block out all of my self-berating thoughts.

I longed for the feeling of fullness in my mouth to the point where I almost had to gasp for air. I wouldn't think about anything, except dislodging the smudges of chocolate chunks on the sides of my fingers, as I carefully picked them out from a dense mufookie. I wanted to stop *thinking,* and chewing helped make the world disappear. It was an endless cycle that was also my deepest and dirtiest secret.

I would spend at least half of my days planning what to eat and when to eat. My other down time was spent on researching and comparing myself to models on Facegram.

"You have no discipline! You're such a failure! Now you've ruined the chance to be a pound less tomorrow!" were words ingrained in my daily mantra.

The system is not only a mindset, but a way of life. Every time I would restrict, every time I would binge, every time I decided to hate myself, I supported the system mandated by Mirror Mania. MM still rules our fifty-thousand-resident city of Speculo, where body weight is viewed as a person's most valuable asset. Every resident is assigned a specific body weight range and if they go above or below, the consequences can be limitless.

* * *

"Writing in your little diary again?" Shojan's sandy brown hair intersects the view of the top of my red moleskin journal.

"At least I'm productive with my feelings," I retort, sticking my nose in the air.

"Right. If that's what you wanna call it, Miss. I Can't Ever Let Things Go," Shojan mocks me.

Barging in from my open doorway, Shojan squints at the creamy, unopened envelope on my desk.

"Man, I can't believe they still hand deliver these things." He rubs his thumb across the mahogany MM stamp on the envelope, while tilting his squarish head.

Though my fingers dwindle around my stationery pen, the thoughts inside of me continue to flow. I used to *love* the system. Like everyone else, I was *obsessed* with the number on the scale. It defined me. It engaged me. It limited me. It excited me. It was my *leader.* Every decision, every thought, every time I needed to put food in my mouth was driven by that number.

"Sooo, are you gonna open this thing? Or just stare at it until it makes you go crazy? Oh wait, that's probably already happened by now, hasn't it?" Shojan says with a hearty chuckle.

"Shut up! I just feel anxious, okay?" I say, quickly turning my head away from him.

"I understand Ropa, but you've grown a lot. You can handle this. I know you want this, otherwise you wouldn't have even applied," he explains.

Heaving a sigh, I look to the empty hallway—glimpsing at Shojan's feeble attempt of closing my light oak door behind him. It seems dimmer when the lights are off, yet more elegant, lit with the scent of Mom's non-GMO lavender honeysuckle candles.

"C'mon, you got this. I know you wanna open it alone, but I'm still here to talk if you need to," Shojan softly remarks.

"I know, but it's just Mirror Mania stuff like usual. My body weight defines pretty much everything about me… I hate that. I can't stop, but I can't pretend it's not happening. What difference does knowing make? The Influencers at MM have all the power," I admit, restlessly fidgeting my legs around. He's had to listen to me talk about this forever.

"You haven't opened it yet, man. You don't even know if you got into the program. Stop this spiral thinking, you're better than that," Shojan reassuringly pats my shoulder.

"I know, I know."

"Thanks. I really needed this,"

Mussing his sandy locks up and down, Shojan grins in support and slowly walks backward.

"Poof! I'm out," he mimics.

"Nerd."

I carefully uncross my legs, while staring at myself in my mirror ceiling, painted with invisible protective plexiglass that Dad installed because I tried to break it two years ago after a fight with Mom about how I've gained weight. Making my way to my floating vanity that is coffee colored today, my dry fingers gingerly tighten around the envelope. I can feel its weightless contents begging me to discover what remains inside. I vehemently shake it around, instantly flashing back to a very distinct checkup I had at Mirror Mania's infamous Body Imaging Centre two years ago.

"Remember, if you're over your maximum body weight or under your minimum body weight, you are not allowed the same opportunities as being in the ideal range," my assigned Influencer, Anastasia, would say every year I had my appointment.

Her contacts change with each season: green glitter, tie-dye purple and silver, one time even a checkered pattern. Her hair color has always remained the same since she's been my Influencer, however: a boring chocolate brown color with a singular white streak on the right side of her head.

That particular year I was even more insecure than usual. It was the year of my last checkup with Influencer Anastasia because I could select anyone I wanted after turning eighteen. What I despised even more about this checkup was that I had gained over 30 pounds since my last one. The glowing mirrors covering the whole interior of Mirror Mania's lobby fooled me: I didn't know which appearance to believe, or rather, which one to unconditionally love. I dreaded how Influencer Anastasia was going to observe me like a specimen she was about to dissect, pinching my stomach and armpit fat, while giddily examining my cellulite with a magnifying glass.

Influencer Anastasia's patient room has always been just a plain white room with absolutely nothing in it, except an old-fashioned scale. No digital scale or a BMI meter; it is just a simple, functional bodyweight reader. I remember standing in the room, fearing Anastasia's boring hair of all things. I can still feel her bizarre looking eyes judging every single inch of my tubby, flabby body. The bright mirror door fizzled, instantly revealing a pair of gold sparkly colored eyes.

"Ropashna, nice to see you again. Get on the scale, please," Influencer Anastasia said, sizing me up and down.

"Wow. You're 30 pounds over your maximum point. You've been at the perfect midpoint for most of your life, so what... what happened?" she said with her furrowed eyebrows concentrating on the big red number.

I feel my shoulders shrug and my droopy eyes falling to the bleak white tiled floor. I'm five feet and four inches: 115 was my assigned *minimum* point and 140 was my assigned *maximum* point. I'd managed to stay on track between 120 and 130 since I'd been eight years old; my pursuit of perfection quickly became a part of everyday life. The pressure to conform, the "oohs" and "ahhs," the approval—I loved it all, I needed it.

"I just... I just can't do it anymore. I don't want to spend hours looking at menus, thinking that if I'm 1 pound over my perfect midpoint that I'm a worthless failure. I don't want to log everything I eat all the time! I can't live like this anymore!" the words poured out of me, while my body filled itself with heat pulsing through my veins.

"Right. So, the solution is to eat yourself out of existence? Don't you want to be an Influencer one day? You've always talked about interning here. How are you going to get in? You know that one of the requirements to even be considered is to maintain your perfect midpoint weight," Influencer Anastasia condescendingly taunted, revealing her oddly pointed teeth.

"I'm done with it. I deserve to be free. Watch me thrive on Facegram and I'll get into the Mirror Mania Internship Program regardless of my weight," I remember saying with extreme certainty, intently staring at her.

Not waiting for my results, I remember storming off, completely ignoring whatever Influencer Anastasia wanted to guilt me with. Even though that stupid checkup was two years ago, it was the day when I knew I needed to make a change for myself, not what I had been told by Mirror Mania my entire life.

Fluttering my eyes back to the envelope in front of me, my lip twitches and the seal rips. It all happens suddenly. Out falls a red flavor tag and before I can manage to overthink, I flip it onto my tongue, feeling it satisfyingly dissolve. On my wrist, my tech button blares, instantly projecting a holographic message from Mirror Mania. My eyes mechanically skim over the message, searching for those distinct, but very heavy words. I acknowledge some of the extra fluff describing some logistics on Intern Orientation, uniform skin suits, and body weight requirements. And then I finally find it, repeating it over and over again:

"Congratulations, Ropashna. You have been accepted," signed *The Head Influencer.*

Suddenly, the ability to begin destroying Mirror Mania once and for all is now completely real.

CHAPTER 2

NEVER FORGET: DESLIN

———

It was like everyone could see how much I weighed, as if my forehead labeled itself with that all defining number. They would look at me and laugh. Not many people would say anything to my face, but that was the worst part. Instead, they would take pictures of me and put them in group chats or make memes. Because that's how bullying works when you're past the age of six.

"Ha. Did you see what Deslin posted?"

"Nope, but he probably looks like what I ate for dinner yesterday."

"Lumpy, moldy protein-injected potatoes? Just look at his arms, man!"

I remember every time I would look at Facegram, I would feel so anxious, questioning if it was worth posting for the rest of the world to see. Even though I'm a guy, I always felt like I was an insecure teenage girl that was born with attention coded in her DNA.

For most of my life, I had been overweight by 30 pounds, according to Mirror Mania standards. Every checkup, Aama would constantly argue with my assigned Influencer Anastasia, urging that I was indeed a healthy boy who loved to eat her cooking too much. While that was accurate, she more so knew it was because she didn't know how else to cheer me up when I would come home, greeting her with an indifferent face only to immediately retreat to my room.

"Oi! Desloo. Aren't you going to eat dinner? I made your favorite Contra dish! Spicy garlic fish and fried yams," Aama would chime.

Basking in my airy beanbag, I would punch it from all of my pent-up rage. Each punch was for every name and stare, but the black, grainy texture would barely puff down.

So what if I'm 30 pounds over my maximum point? I'm a big guy. So what, *Jimmy*? I'm not cool enough to hang out with you now just because of a fucking number.

"Deslinnnn! You need to eat!" She'd insistently remind me.

With a growling stomach and raging mind, I just needed it all to stop. When it was just me, Aama, and food, I was accepted. She would see me burping with a full belly, and we would laugh together because all she ever wanted was to see me smile. What at first seemed like iridescent bliss would suddenly evaporate, after the person who was even more damaging to me than my so-called friends would walk in my room.

"Hey, piggo. Haven't eaten enough? All you do is eat, eat, eat," Papa would say, shaking his head in disgust as if I was an unrecognizable breed of his blood.

"Let him eat, Ubili. He is a growing boy," Aama would try and stick up for me.

Every place in Speculo has a scanner that reads a person's body weight as they enter. Large and extravagant corporations refuse to allow overweight or underweight people inside, even if it's just by a few deviating pounds from your assigned maximum or minimum points. Other businesses are more lenient.

Back in my overweight days, the only places I could get into were pop-up shops. Even when I would go out with Aama or Papa, they would be allowed in most of the time at whichever place we went to, and I had to sit outside patiently waiting. I remember celebrating Crossfitmas one year crying outside the giant stadium, having two Mirror Mania droids accompany me.

"Deslin. From Contra. You are 30 pounds over maximum point. You may not enter," one of the droids with a chipped mirror arm kept repeating.

"Yes, I get it. I'm useless," I miserably affirmed to myself, glaring at my reflection in the other droid's chromatic ab accentuated stomach.

"WOOO! UBILI, THE BEST BEAUTY BIO SPACE INFLUENCER IN ALL OF SPECULO WINS AGAIN!" The announcer of the stadium blared.

Of course, he was winning. My dad was the perfect one; everyone in Speculo knew him. I was just the talentless, fat ass son. Almost every day someone would find out what seemed to be the most interesting fact about me.

"Influencer Ubili is *your* dad? Dang! Bro, I bet he sees all kinds of chicks asking for some ass implants."

"Really? Ubili is so cool man! You're so lucky you have an Influencer as a dad. He must be the best dad ever."

The expectations of everyone else, along with the expectations of my dad were just too overbearing.

I had nothing better to do than fill my head with negativity: my parents don't even want to be near me, why can't I just be normal like everyone else? I always felt alone, unloved, unworthy. I missed Crossfitmas almost every year, birthday parties, amusement parks, everything that a high school boy should never have to watch from standing out in the cold and darkness.

Papa, on the other hand, had gotten frustrated with my depressive attitude and told me to start exercising if I wanted to stop getting made fun of.

"If you want to stand up for yourself, you need to be able to physically stand up in the first place. How do you even plan to get into the Mirror Mania Influencer internship program?" I remember him telling me the year before university.

At first, I raged some more. I was bullied at school but felt like I was bullied at home even more. He was right. I knew I needed to make a change, so I took my dad's advice and decided to jump in the pool. The local pool refused to let me in because I was too overweight, so I decided to swim in a dirty, mucky lake nearby. It was summer and I had no friends. I had absolutely nothing to lose, except the extra weight Mirror Mania deemed that I had.

I hated MM. I hated how Papa was an Influencer. I hated everything about the system. It made me have nobody to hang out with. It made me feel like I didn't deserve to eat the delicious, packaged crap that's sold at the pop-up shops or go electric surfing like the other eighteen-year old guys who had abs and probably because they ate chickpea mac and pine nut cheese all the time.

So, the water became my safe haven. I remember taking swimming lessons as a kid until the facility banned me for being a fat ass. Surprisingly, I still had some muscle memory; my hatred toward MM served as motivation. As much as it felt like my arms were moving through goo, requiring all of my strength to pick myself up, I knew it was time to fight back.

Nine months have passed since then, and I've lost 50 pounds. I can actually see my ribcage, arm veins, and bulging muscles. I finally feel confident like those guys on Facegram with their oiled up, hairless torsos. I love when my shitty bullies and so-called friends try to follow me on Facegram because they probably would have never thought that I would look like this now. I feel like I can even stand up to Papa too because he actually respects me, especially after receiving my acceptance letter.

I'll have to suck up and bring the Influencers their protein and collagen-infused cold brew coffees every morning, but at least I'll be inside. And that's all I need to be able to see how I can destroy this shitty system once and for all.

◊

CHAPTER 3

INTERN ORIENTATION: ROPASHNA

———

It's finally here: intern orientation. I'm surprised I even made it to the in-person round. My tech button's alarm vibrates through my wrist, dispatching a clenching jolt of energy throughout my pear-shaped body. It's six in the morning, but outside looks the same as it did the moment that I shut my eyes last night: serene darkness freckled with shiny bullets darting around and enthusiastic white droids marching their sculpted legs.

The first thing I do is take a gigantic shit and weigh myself three times for accuracy: 160.4. One of the minimum requirements to be accepted as an Influencer Intern is to be at the midpoint of your assigned weight range. That's why I'm so surprised, considering I'm now 20 pounds over my maximum. Then again, everyone eats up Facegram these days. I do have fifty-thousand followers, mainly though my body positive posts and controversial articles, so I *guess* that might be a reason to why I was accepted.

"Ropaaashna! You need to GO!" Mom's annoyingly strong shrill pierces through the crack of my bathroom door.

I scrunch my waist-length wavy hair with organic grown cardamom herbal oil and effortlessly slink into my black spandex uniform that highlights all of my curves. Coasting down the stairs, my hands feed me whatever I rummage through in the fridge's cobalt blue gel: a breakfast of collagen-protein-infused bananas, nitrate-free crunch clusters, and fat-free avocado. I quickly rush out the door before Mom can tell me my cleavage is showing too much.

Of course, she gets luckier than me and is waiting by our seven-foot-tall dark cherry front door. Dressed in a forest green salwar and kohl drooping from her eyes, Mom greets me with sharply raised eyebrows that seem drawn on from being so dark and cleanly shaped.

"Hm! Where do you think you're going looking like that, missy?" she says under the dimly lit room.

"You just told me I have to go! I don't have time for this right now, Mom!" I say a little bit louder than intended.

"Can't you just put something on underneath? Why do you have to have your boobies popping out?" She doesn't give up.

"It's fine! It barely shows. My bullet is here, gotta go!" I grin and close the door also a bit louder than intended.

My moody combination skin is hit with a slight breeze in the humid morning of Juneria. Juneria is my favorite month: not too humid and not freezing. A driver droid arrives in a silver bullet. Everyone rides in bullets nowadays. They're efficient cars shaped like a compact gun bullet. They're more efficient because droids haven't been coded to drive other types of vehicles yet. People who actually miss driving still drive those big vehicles with steering wheels you actually control yourself. I've always wanted to learn how to drive stick shift, but Mom thinks such a dated skill is only suited for those way too below or above their midpoints. She's always cared so much about what others think. No wonder she never misses her daily macro goals.

Within seven minutes, I'm dropped off at the chromatic steps to the gorgeously intimidating Mirror Mania. It's surrounded by mirrors on all sides, so that you never forget what you look like. Its large block of perfectly divided mirror squares attracts girls and guys about my age bustling inside, most of them stopping at the mirror exterior to take belfies (butt selfies) or checking whose jawline looks sharper than the other. I sigh, run my hands through my coarse black hair, and step inside.

I've only ever visited the lobby and the Body Imaging Centre for my yearly checkups at Mirror Mania. A swirling staircase lined with clean, white droids and bright spotlights embraces the open space, but looks crowded from the thirty nervous and extremely self-conscious intern applicants inside, who most likely want to actually be influencers. Meanwhile, I just want their power, but I know have to do the thing I used to be perfect at and now despise pretend to be like everyone else.

In placement of meaningful conversation, the other interns seem to be comparing waist measurements, exchanging Facegrams, and shaking their legs out of nervousness. Even in the lobby, there are mirrors everywhere. There are even skinny ones to make you look slimmer and wide ones to make you look chubby. There are tiny ones to inspect the nittiest details of your body. I hate this place. I'm considered fat only because of some stupid guidelines, but I don't care. I thought I would feel so insecure because of that, but everyone is too occupied with themselves to see my bra bulge or nonexistent thigh gap. I honestly don't even look like I'm 160 pounds at five-foot-one. It's because I have quite a lot of muscle, but I do enjoy calling myself thick to make myself feel better.

While I feel my throat clenching and my head slowly burning, I simultaneously feel someone's eyes on me. Of all people, it's a guy. A hot, chocolate-skinned, hazel-eyed, ringlet-curled-hair boy. How exotic, exciting, and *distracting!* I shouldn't return his gaze, but it's so hard not to. He's across the room just examining me. I look at him, he smiles, I look away and look back quickly. He just laughs. That's the thing about arrogant boys that seem confident. They're hard to resist, yet you know it's in your best interests to stay away. He begins to walk over; I see his chiseled cheekbones and outlined shoulder muscles. Why would he want *me?*

Suddenly, the hottie halts. An uncharacteristically loud and uncalled for "boom!" captures the room, and out emerge three influencers from the hidden mirror doors on one of the walls. All of them are girls, and they look very similar: some type of brightly highlighted hair, pouty lips, heavy coats of cruelty free mascara, perfectly styled hair and basic white lab coats with their basic names on their implanted breast pockets. Most of the guys in the room stare as if they've succeeded in living their childhood dreams, and I'm pretty sure I see at least one of them secretly jacking off.

Scanning the room some more, I eventually realize the girls around me could all be related to the three influencers at the front of the room. They're mainly all white and have the same athletic, square body type. There are a few black girls and what seems to be other brown girls, but other than that, I'm in the minority. I kind of like it, I guess. I feel different and unique, and I can use that to my advantage. At the same time, I feel eroticized and judged for my hair texture, curvy body type, and darker skin. Even in savvy Speculo, the city where most people ride in the same type of car, inequality of others still continues to exist. Though I was born in Speculo, my roots are from Sunare. I don't really know much about it, other than it is a beautiful, dangerous town, just like most culturally rich areas. wonder where the cute, hazel-eyed guy is from. I'm just gonna have to call him Hazel Eyes; he's definitely not from Sunare or even my part of the world.

The influencers introduce themselves with names that aren't as basic as I initially thought: Anastasia, Brecky, and Jeenz. I was actually expecting them to just refer to themselves as their Facegram handles. Influencer Jeenz seems to be the most unbothered, yet the most serious of the crew.

"Hello everyone! Congratulations on making it this far! Thank you all for wearing the spandex uniforms we sent you. We wanted to see if your bodies were as perfect as the pictures you post on Facegram! Hehe!" Influencer Anastasia cackles and flutters her creepy rainbow-colored contact eyes.

I shudder at the sound of her unappetizing voice and even more gruesome looking eyes.

"We are going to divide you into three groups to learn about the main sections of Mirror Mania. You will all be paired up with one Influencer per group, for they will guide you around the layout of our beloved palace. There's the Beauty Bio Space, the Body Imaging Centre, and the Communications and Analytics Department," Influencer Jeenz explains.

Great. I wonder who I'll be paired up with.

"Now, everyone listen up! This is random. Ten people per team," Influencer Anastasia starts randomly counting off people with her live sparkly claw-like nails.

I hear my name.

"Rop...ash...nuhhaa? Beauty Bio Space!" Influencer Brecky manages to finally blurt, shaking her pale wrist out of what I assume is stage fright.

Furthest from the entrance of the lobby, Influencer Jeenz holds up a tablet with a flashing GIF with the title "Influencer Jeenz: Beauty Bio Space" in bright, sparkly gold letters. Looking around, faces with glistening sweat and sticky baby hairs paint my view, but one girl particularly catches my eye. She's one of the darker-skinned girls I saw earlier, but her darting eyes and hair petting suggests some insecurity. Before I could engage in any small talk, Influencer Jeenz begins to lead us out to the mirror doors.

"These disguised mirror doors are so confusing!" The darker-skinned girl bumps her smooth shoulder next to me.

"Huh? Oh yeah," I crisply say. I'm not here to make *friends*.

One by one, we all surrender to the mirrors, as our bodies are sucked into a corridor filled with nothing but our reflections and chromatic space.

"State desired location," a metallic voice echoes throughout the corridor.

"Beauty. Bio. Space," Influencer Jeenz responds.

Still in a line behind Influencer Jeenz, we're all lifted up like in some kind of elevator up to the first floor.

"Couldn't we have just taken that spiral staircase thing?" A shrill voice of an intern says.

"Or perhaps you can appreciate how Mirror Mania has access to the most advanced technology in Speculo City," Influencer Jeenz shuts the voice down.

After arriving, the floor transforms into a padded surface. Influencer Jeenz goes first and firmly presses her feet on the floor, prompting a green light to scan her body up and down. The system clicks in a completion noise and states her current body weight: Check! Slight warning. You are two fifths of a pound above your midpoint weight. This could be due to daily fluctuations. However, take caution as necessary."

We all follow. I go last, so nobody hears my data, but I'm still cleared through and allowed to go inside for some reason.

Upon entering, there are stretch mark gels and booty growth creams on floating glass tables with other lotions that seem to be newly developed products that haven't been publicly released yet. There's a black dresser, black plush rugs, and a few black recliner seats.

"This section of the Beauty Bio Space focuses more on pampering. Here, influencers like myself suggest what needs to be changed or enhanced on the client's body. We have all types of products, but none of the cheap crap you find in pop-up shops."

Jeenz then guides us to another corner; there's tweezers, scalpels, nail cutters, extra skin contained in glass cylinders with dark green liquid, and knives of all shapes and sizes.

"I know this part of the room looks much gorier, but I find it to be the most advancing. This area is what I like to call the Plastics corner. All types of operations can be performed here: nose jobs, lip plumping, implants, whole face transformations, liposuction, and other surgeries. A new one just came out actually. It's called Defining. Only our most skilled Influencers trained in the Beauty Bio Space perform surgeries; Defining is when a client wants a specific body part to appear more muscular or shapely. The Influencer then removes excess fat from the body part and permanently tattoos defining lines to accentuate it, giving a natural look."

I wonder if Hazel Eyes has gotten that done. I honestly don't know what to make of all this behind the scenes crap. It's all so fascinating that people spend so much time and effort trying to be someone else, someone other than themselves. It's more captivating to see that someone helps another not be themselves for a living. As I'm in lost in thought, my hands sway to the side, clashing a bottle of leftover collagen injectors on one of the lab tables. A blonde chick who probably posts what she eats in a day to complement her daily lower body workout on Facegram glares her bulging blue eyes at me.

The darker-skinned girl smiles a bit, and Influencer Jeenz just glances our way, while continuing to show everyone around. The group makes their way to the largest portion of the Beauty Bio Space. It resembles old factory conditions with twitching droids that seem to be drained or turned off, crushed white pills, old formula sheets with mysterious liquid stains, test tubes with purple liquid that's still bubbling, and a sink for water gloves.

"Woah! Are those water glov-"

Influencer Jeenz eyes pierce through one of the loud-mouth interns trying to interrupt her, but within a second her face returns to an unfazed poker face.

"Everyone, here are the infamous water gloves that Mirror Mania is quite famous for developing. These are gloves that form under water and freeze on your hands. Influencers take pills to allow their bodies to regulate their temperatures, so they don't freeze to death. Essentially, they were developed because Beauty Bio Space nerds wanted to test if they could manipulate human body temperature regulation," Influencer Jeenz explains with not much interest or amusement. She seems bored with it all, as if she's desensitized to Mirror Mania's crazy inventions.

The background music continues in "oohs" and "ahhs" from the interns.

"The Beauty Bio Space is where all the magic happens. New medicines, weight loss aids, chemicals for products, and plastic constructions for surgery developments are all produced here. You guys have probably heard about our most popular Influencer here, Influencer Ubili. His son is actually one of the interns present today as well," Jeenz talks at us as if she's a droid with her lack of voice inflection.

Finally, we sink back into the mirror corridor. The second group passes us by and of course, my eyes land on Hazel Eyes.

CHAPTER 4

THE PLAN: DESLIN

———

This place is filled with everyone I ever wanted to be when I was kid, yet they all hated me, so they can all go suck my dick.

Honestly, it doesn't matter anymore because I already know I can flex on all of them. Just look at my Facegram account: undeniable abdominal muscles, cutting cheekbones, and defined arms all proven by the thirsty, fine ass girls in my comments. I really thought today was going to be as boring and predictable as it gets, but a familiar terrain of flowing black hair and golden skin entertains my view. As my group and Influencer Anastasia make our way to the Body Imaging Centre, I see her again.

Her shape seems familiar. Nah, she definitely wasn't someone I've slept with before. I would have remembered. My Facegram feed has often been flooded with images of her round face and plump lips saturated with a funky red or pink. Her captions are usually all kinds of controversial topics about body discrimination in Speculo. Why in the world would she be *here?* My eyes keep looking for something, trying to lock into hers for at least more than a second, as if that would help me remember her name or Facegram handle. Her wide pupils keep flickering at me, while she fidgets to adjust the top of her busty skinsuit. Her extra cushioning seems comforting to me. Maybe, she's struggling like how I did.

Her brown, sparkly eyes move in my direction, almost bribing me into telling her my name. Why am I so drawn to a girl that I've only seen on Facegram? I've seen hundreds of the baddest chicks, but this one just seems different. I gotta give her my Facegram at the very least, but Influencer Anastasia and the others have passed through the corridor already, so I'm the only one left that they're waiting for.

I feel my body weight cement onto the pads, whooshing me into an ambient circular room with tons of off-white doors that are just check-up rooms. In the center, a large glass cylinder scanner bobs up and down, beaming with bright yellow sparks. A messy bunch of red roses, that are actually a lanky guy's head of hair, curiously and clumsily imprints his hand on the clear glass.

"Scanning. Perfect. Midpoint. Access. To. Any. Room," a high-tech, clear voice states.

"Yes!" the redhead jumps up and down as if he just reached another one thousand followers on Facegram.

My lips smush up to hide my amusement, still ensuring my cheekbones are a topic amongst the girls near Influencer Anastasia who's going off about what's hot in Juneria's body shape trends. The opposite side of Anastasia is completely packed with protruding live frames containing an unlimited array of digital images fizzling from one to the next: aesthetic proportions of well-cooked biceps, ink-scratched formulas to achieve the perfect midpoint weight, neon-colored macronutrient charts, low-carb recipe research, and of course, printouts of Facegram transformations from Speculo's finest Influencer Ubili.

"Welcome to what Mirror Mania is basically known for to Speculo City! Everyone in Speculo is *required* to get their yearly checkup, so clients of all ages are assigned to an influencer and all that. We use our own background knowledge and Facegram expertise to determine the client's lowest weight, highest weight, and midpoint weight. You guys already know. We also give recommendations on how to achieve a specific body type, assign new diets, and blah, blah," Influencer Anastasia says in between mindless chews of fat-blasting gum that changes color according to how much of an effect has taken place.

How can she be so unbothered about being a reason for a destructive self-esteem? Older thin tablet posters are scrolled up against the creamy walls behind Influencer Anastasia. Obviously, the Best Booty Package is where my eyes dart toward.

"Clients pay just forty dollars a month for booty building shakes, meal plans, and booty growth exercises. We do the research for you," its headlines reads.

The bold pink lettering and grainy images of blonde tanned chicks means the poster definitely had some dated advertising techniques. *Huh.* The one thing that hasn't changed is that people need to be told how to eat and what to eat, as if they've forgotten what hunger actually feels like. I know I did.

I've been visiting this place ever since I was a kid, but all these Influencers do is spur a bunch of bullshit. The only thing that actually transformed my body was myself and figuring out what worked for me. The rest of the Body Imaging Centre swirls with lightly furnished waiting areas. A floating glass table scatters itself with what seems to appear as red and black pages. A few of the interns flock over to the mysterious pages or what seems to be some type of magazine on thin black tablets. I don't really care about all that girly junk, but I do know that Mirror Mania's own magazine contains the newest developments, newest experiments, and newest technologies.

"Ah, yeah. You guys found the Mirror Mania Magazine. It's cool or whatever! Whatever fad you guys want, you can find it in there. Just sit down and swipe away, like spending hours on Facegram," Influencer Anastasia comments.

When I get fully accepted into the program, I am going to change all this fluffy content to actual, scientific-backed evidence, not just some *proof* based on the number of followers from a sexy, honey-dripping lips influencer has on Facegram. I feel angry but motivated when looking around me because it reminds me of how I thought I was never good enough, according to the poster of a man that's a supposed saint to Speculo.

"Yo! When we gonna go to the last section already? I'm getting hungry, man!" a familiar obnoxious curly head of hair shouts.

As if on cue, Influencer Anastasia flicks the lights off, and we head to the last section of Mirror Mania: the Communications and Analytics Department. It seems miniature compared to the other areas, yet oddly cozy. Half of the room divides itself with sparkling glossy doors, opening to a space with tablets, large projections of Facegram user data, and overused black bean bag chairs. It seems a bit too nerdy for me.

"Damn! So much writing. Looks like a crazy exhibition with all these article ideas, layouts, and marketing. Where's the cool stuff, ya know what I mean!" The redhead shimmies over to me.

"For sure, bro," I cut him off before the conversation goes into some hippie, artsy territory.

It's all too girly for me. I feel like these people don't do much, so no wonder why this room is the smallest of them all.

Then, my hands trace over the fingerpencils on the floating work desks, losing myself in the remarkable technology of it all: my finger molds into a long, perfectly sharpened pencil. *Damn.* I guess it's not horrible down here.

"I never said you guys could look around yet. Anyway, welcome to the Communications and Analytics Department, aha. Influencer Brecky is in charge of this place, but she's still in the lobby, aha. Clients can receive advice on absolutely *anything* having to do with Facegram over here. Grow your Facegram following through algorithm manipulation, follower bribery, managing Influencer profiles, profile aesthetic lessons, and promoting Mirror Mania products. The communications team focuses on ghost copywriting, planning virtual neighborhood events, and creating our quarterly Mirror Mania Magazine," Influencer Anastasia oddly elaborates, as if she doesn't want Influencer Brecky to feel bad for not being there.

"Wait! What kind of events does Mirror Mania hold? Are they only exclusive to Mirror Mania Influencers?" a plastic barbie, with awkwardly stretched hips from our intern group inquires.

"Oh yeahhh. For the most part, events are only for Mirror Mania staff. Other events are to empower the public to follow weight guidelines, weigh themselves daily, and various *empowerment* projects," Influencer Anastasia emphasizes, deviously twisting the dead ends of her dyed hair.

What is she hiding? She seems a lot smarter than she leads on. I'm so tired of touring this damn place; I just want to get on with beating everyone at whatever it is that we have to do, to finally make it into the internship program. Noticing the time, Influencer Anastasia herds us all back to the lobby to reunite with the other interns and Influencers.

I see her again, with those dark, bouncy waves and naturally thick lashes. I feel like such an infatuated idiot by even noticing those details. I'm so sick of the unrealistic blemish-free skin and filtered anime eyes that her realness feels *refreshing.*

"Checking out the new meat, eh?" The redhead bumps into me again.

"What's it to you, man? Can't you tell I'm not interested?" I spit back.

"Chill, hot head. Just trying to be friendly. The name's Jrelito," he says with too much rolling, but not out of expecting me to say my name back.

The room bustles with the other groups all looking to the front of the lobby for direction from the three Influencers Anastasia, Brecky, and Jeenz. Jrelito's eyes maneuver over to a few droids walking by, holding up mirrors for two Influencer guys. *Huh,* I didn't know we'd have a gay dude in our cohort.

"Gather around! We hope that you all enjoyed exploring Mirror Mania, but now it's time to prove that you belong here. Only twenty-one of you will be selected, so listen carefully and try your best!"Anastasia speaks first.

Influencer Brecky finally speaks up. She adjusts her glasses and clears her throat, revealing her squeaky voice.

"This is your task. It's quite simple, really. The first twenty-one we pick are in because, uh, we have three sections! No exceptions! The task is to develop a marketing plan for a sixteen-year-old, maximum weight girl who needs to be convinced to buy cellulite cream."

Marketing isn't my expertise, but I know all about that cellulite cream. Back home, my dad has a whole stash of that grey goopy shit in his hidden supplies room. I got this, *Brecky.* What kind of name is *Brecky,* anyway? Maybe her parents thought Becky was too basic and Brekkie would be another basic way to say breakfast, so they decided to spell her name in a clever way. Around me, girls with black beanies pair up, the very few numbers of guys look around and shrug, staying in their own spaces, and of course, she's sitting on a floating mirror saucer. It's the perfect opportunity to talk to her; I'm sure she'll need the help, anyway.

"I know you've been waiting, so thanks for your patience, I smirk.

"Waiting? Sorry, but I'm too busy trying to beat you and everyone else that I don't even have the *time* to stress over some random guy," she retorts.

"Hm. Feisty. I like it. Well, we can bicker later. But if you actually want to get in, I suggest that you listen to me," I say.

She rolls her eyes at me, but a sarcastic "hm" invites me to move closer to her. She's not from Contra, which is where I was born and raised. My family and I moved here for me to receive a better education about four years ago. I miss Contra because a lot of my family and friends are still there. We are of the darker skin types, eat extremely spicy food, eat fried plantain as an afternoon snack, and listen to songs with a lot of drums in it.

"Listen, the influencers want a plan that will *influence*. Everyone is probably gonna do the same thing and talk about how much better life will be without cellulite or how the girl's stretch marks will magically go away after one use."

"I wasn't going to do that, but alright. I'm listening," she opens up more.

"They want emotion and feeling; they want to empathize, not sell to the sixteen-year-old. Use that strategy and you'll definitely get in," I say, lifting my head up and staring right into her glowing face.

She opens her mouth only a little bit, but that's enough to give me satisfaction. I quickly wave over a helper droid to give me a scratch tablet, so I can start on my own plan. As I begin sashaying my fingers on the blank surface, a lace of black hair peaks over my shoulder.

"I know we're supposed to have separate plans, but I just wanted to know... what you're planning to do... exactly," she says, managing to nervously stutter every few syllables.

It's kind of cute.

"Well, I'm pretty sure that's cheating. Focus on yourself, but a tip is that I know how the girl feels from personal experience. She wants to feel confident and accepted, so I would just talk to her and make her trust you. Only then I would bring up the cream. It's all about emotion," I explain.

I watch her eyes soften for a second, maybe out of empathy.

"Well, what a softie you are! I think I got it now," her cute, loose curls bob up and down.

We get back to working and my hands and brain feed each other so fast that I don't even notice the little hottie beside me run off. *That's not the priority right now.* After I'm done and ready to present my work, there's already two brave people in a single line. I feel a bit salty that I wasn't the first one finished, but I doubt the influencers will accept the ones in front of me anyway. The first contender is a petite, green-eyed girl. *Too timid.*

"Well, we can use magazines and celebrity endorsements. Teenage girls love that!" She squeals even louder than Influencer Brecky.

The bobblehead shaking and pursing of overly plump lips of all three Influencers send the girl away with her dainty head looking at the floor, her face gradually adorning the chromatic floor with tear droplets. Then, to my surprise, it's the girl. That's where she ran off to! My ears spy to overhear her name and see if my tips actually worked. Worst case, they were a great excuse to flirt with her, at least.

"Hi, I'm Ropashna. It would be effective if we analyze the sixteen-year old's Facegram data to figure out her likes and interests. Then, we could target her through getting her friends involved with buying the cream and promote posts about the cream that target her through her specific interests," she sophisticatedly explains.

The influencers have mixed reactions, though. Anastasia nods with approval, Jeenz smiles, but Brecky squints a bit, most likely out of comprehension issues. After a few moments of silence, I want to speak up and save Ropashna.

To my surprise, a unison of voices exclaims, "You're in! Congratulations to be the first Influencer Intern in this year's Mirror Mania Internship Program."

Damn, those were words that I thought I would be the one to hear first. Her silky hair glides over her shoulders, as she winks back at me before sinking into the mirror doors. I step up to hand over my work on the tablet and pitch my idea next.

"It's about emotion. I was overweight once and I hated myself. A sixteen-year-old just wants to wake up every day and feel comfortable in her own skin. I would tell her that the cream won't solve all of her problems, but it sure can help her. My tactic is based on combining pure truth and emotion: basic persuasion."

The influencers are shocked. It makes me feel so good. My ego is soaring beyond space because it's usually at the sky. I bet they all think I'm hot shit. Speaking of, Influencer Jeenz is kinda cute.

"You're Influencer Ubili's son, correct?" Jeenz says, looking up from the black tablet screen.

Her piercing, lovely green eyes don't make his name sound as bad as it usually does.

"Indeed I am. Learned a lot from the man," I promptly say.

"Well, when you go home, be sure to tell him that you're officially part of the Internship program. Congratulations. You deserve it," Influencer Jeenz announces.

"Thank you so much! I definitely will," I say, attempting to conceal my bursting excitement.

Stepping into the mirror doors of approval, my body relaxes into the corridor to be greeted by Ropashna's stunning behind. I miss the communal feeling of Contra, but Speculo City girls really have grown on me, if you know what I mean. I only like the naturally thick ones, not that plastic shit my dad digs his face into every day.

"So, my tips worked then, I assume," I whisper behind her.

She jumps and her caramel hue lightens a little, slightly replaced with a tinge of rosiness.

"Well, I guess they weren't *that* bad," she grins.

"You're something else, aren't you?" I say with a sexy head tilt.

Three other buff guys all stumble in and a black chick linking arms with a tall, snowy looking girl prance in, clamoring the corridor with flirting and laughing.

"This girl-to-guy ratio is insane," I press Ropashna.

"Probably because all the guys are afraid that they'll be called pussy or gay on Facegram," Ropashna snorts.

She's kind of funny too. I like it. I used to care a lot about that title, but then I decided to actually grow up. We're all in university. We're all adults. Plus, a pussy is stronger than a penis, so I don't mind being called that most of the time. Sparking through, Jrelito's messy, red hair now bound together by a loose bun makes an appearance.

"Hey brother. Which department are you joining?" Jrelito questions.

"Beauty Bio Space all the way. And you?" I ask back.

"Let's go! What's your name, man?" he finally tests me.

It's easy to be a dick, but I feel like I'm contradicting myself when I act fake because it's that same attitude that I'm trying so hard to rebel against.

"The name's Deslin," I say, shaking his oddly clammy hands. This dude is *weird*.

After the rest of the accepted interns arrive, Influencers Anastasia, Jeenz, and Brecky all lead us back to the lobby. Ropashna, Jrelito, and I all walk near one another. Maybe, taking place is going to be a lot more difficult than I thought.

"Congratulations everyone! Please separate yourselves by the interest of your department and enjoy the light refreshments. Feel free to leave whenever. The first day is tomorrow at seven in the morning!" Influencer Brecky screeches.

I watch Ropashna drift over to the other side of the lobby, while I sit with Jrelito. My dry throat quenches with a gob of seaweed water packed with twelve multivitamins for ultimate health that I didn't know were missing from my diet until Mirror Mania said it was. Jrelito's mouth captivates itself with a few pieces of dry, beige pieces of freeze-dried dandelion root flour cookies. I miss Cheetos and double chocolate muffins from my favorite pop-up stores. I turn my head in the opposite direction of Jrelito's vacuum mouth blowing pieces of food everywhere. To my surprise, I watch Ropashna leave her Communications and Analytics Department group to plop those curvy legs right next to me.

"Damn, seaweed water? Trying to lose some weight, eh?" she jokes, yet presses a nerve.

My face sucks inside so hard that my teeth clench on top of my inner cheeks. The words from my mouth unleash like a hunter shooting at the closest moving vertebrae out of necessary hunger.

"Aren't you supposed to be the one doing that? I'm honestly even surprised you made it, miss chubs," I immediately regret the words as soon as they fly out.

Why am I so sensitive? I'm the one that decided to help her, after all. This is what happens when you grow up thinking you'll always be ugly. *Pussy.*

"Wow. I wanted to properly introduce myself, but clearly your ego can't handle it."

She whips her hair in my face and exits. I admire her ass as she walks out with her oddly, adorable feet.

CHAPTER 5

THE COMMUNICATIONS AND ANALYTICS DEPARTMENT: ROPASHNA

After Hazel Eyes or whatever his name is basically called me fat, I've been avoiding him. Surprisingly, Influencer Brecky has made that quite easy with all of the work it takes to create a magazine and all that.

"Uhh...alright everyone! I know that the Communications and Analytics Department isn't the trendiest or highly *technological* area of Mirror Mania, but we are still very much needed," Influencer Brecky says with a sense of enthusiasm that doesn't seem to capture the attention of the other interns.

Instead some of the girls and guys bump their elbows and giggle from messing around with the floating glass tablets, free tech button syncing, and [the] completely toxin free paper laying around their work desks. My eyes wander to a perky, curious looking girl wearing notoriously bright purple colored contacts. Her fully weighted brown ringlets stay contained in two low ponytails; she notices my eyes scanning her.

"Well, as you all get situated here, I want you guys to start brainstorming ideas on what we can do for the next Mirror Mania Magazine Issue! We only publish in print once a year, but all of our single articles, interviews, and features are always offered digitally," Influencer Brecky says, as if she's trying to pitch us into staying in this area for our internships.

"BROOO! We should include a feature about that one dude who's like…300 pounds *above* his maximum. We could include detailed pictures and quotes about how shitty his life is, all that. It would be such a sick piece, man. So many jokes," a random guy with jagged lime green highlighted hair hollers from the desks.

Brecky's doughy face smiles, with half of it taken up by her shining white teeth that sparkle under the shimmery lighting, but her voice depicts a deep disdain with the random intern's proposed idea.

"Anyone else?" Brecky asks. She tilts her head and adjusts her thick, crimson-colored frames.

Pacing around the squeaky sheeny floors, Brecky's eyes waver around my reflection, while her stance remains still on the floating, chrome pad. A petite figure with pointy tails joins the view. I turn toward everyone else.

"I was thinking, maybe we could do something different. Maybe, we could talk about the insecurities that people above their high points and people below their low points *feel*. We could do features on stories describing their everyday experiences, injustices, and the pressure they experience to be at their midpoint," I say.

The room gasps and then falls quiet with stares and raised eyebrows as a response. My spine and shoulders push forward.

"Welllll… that's not a horrible idea. However, that might just make Mirror Mania look…bad. The point of our magazine is to keep us Influencers at the top, to make sure people are reminded of what kind of perfection they should be aiming for. We are a *lifestyle* magazine, after all," Brecky finally says.

She has a point. I can't be so obvious. It's really hard to pretend that I actually want to write about the latest shitty blemish powder and new experiments all for the *lifestyle* of looking a certain way. A group of the interns messing around earlier huddles together, tapping wrists probably to compare Facegram data and old six pack ab pictures from high school. The curious looking girl smiles and squeaks her loud orange Zoomers toward me, but suddenly turns toward Brecky.

"Well, if I may… Influencer Brecky, I think this girl is on to something! You, yourself, even said that the Communications and Analytics Department isn't really funded, and people think we aren't super useful anymore. This is a fresh perspective. It doesn't make Mirror Mania look bad at all; in fact, it shows that we are supportive. We just endorse a healthy lifestyle," the curious looking girl gushes with an even wilder grin than Influencer Brecky.

That was one hell of a pitch. She seems even more curious now. My mouth frowns in admirable surprise.

"Teach me your technique," I whisper loud enough for the girl to hear, yet quiet enough for Influencer Brecky to dismiss as mumbling from the interns who are only here to enlist the position on their tech button data.

A cute but gut-wrenching giggle emerges from a torso that looks like the dolls I used to play with.

"The name's Zasha. You're from Sunare aren't you?" she asks, somehow establishing a sense of familiarity, as soon as the question exits her dark magenta tainted lips.

"I am. No wonder why we're a good team," I chuckle. Zasha's face suddenly beams, as if I had activated some kind of special feature, like on Facegram when you receive over three thousand likes in thirty minutes and are promoted on the main page.

"Totally! Yes! Wow. I actually moved here a few years ago, but I haven't even met anyone from Sunare! I miss it sooo much," Zasha bursts more than the flavour of a fat-burning, organically grown, lemon-flavored collagen chew.

While we chat, I notice Influencer Brecky pondering Zasha's decently convincing idea.

Gently sighing and clasping her dry talon fingers, she says, "Well! Uh...umm...That is quite unbeatable. Anything to make Mirror Mania look wonderous is worth it. We are everything, the law, the government, so might as well go with an idea that boosts us even more...what was your name again? Zashay? Zoosh? Can I just call you ZeeZee? That's cute, right?"

"It's Zasha, but sure! This is a big step. I'm glad you said yes!" Zasha says.

Instantly, Zasha's legs push up three feet in the air, causing my body to sway with her gravity defying skills. The other interns give half smiles and nods, only because Influencer Brecky notes down their participation points.

Obviously, I'm excited, but I realize I can't trust anyone here, not even this Zasha girl. She seems like she's interested in progressing Mirror Mania, but to what extent? I have to remind myself that I'm here to destroy this place, not to make new friends. Influencer Brecky adjusts her frames.

"Well then, everyone please, um, head to your working desks! It's all been set up for you all. All of your Facegram data has been recorded, so that your desks are customizable and comfortable for maximum productivity! Use each other, obviously being respectful and friendly. We're just brainstorming and if anyone wants to write anything, feel free. I'll...uh... be assigning specific pieces throughout the day that I want featured in the magazine. We only publish this in print once a year, but it's always a huge thing! Um... preparation is key! Okay?" Influencer Brecky says with a lack of assurance in herself, but the room fails to satisfy her, once again.

"Such a mom," an intern mumbles.

"More like a MILF," another intern sarcastically mutters.

"Click! Clack!" The interns' tech buttons bump together.

"Bro, what was that for?" One of them heatedly stands over the other, ready to attack.

"Damn, dude. I can't believe you're over your midpoint by *that* much! Wooww! Hahaha!" The other intern teases.

Brecky awkwardly whistles and quietly backward steps back to her clear glass box office.

"Soo! What's up? What brought you to Mirror Mania?" Zasha immediately starts chatting.

Of course, her seat is next to mine. We're organized by Facegram data and all that. Mirror Mania probably also knows we're both from Sunare.

"Well, I just knew that I wanted to be an intern because Mirror Mania has changed my life. The system is part of who I am," I say.

I mean, I'm not lying. I never said I couldn't have any kind of fun while I'm here.

"Interestinggg. I came because I've always dreamt of being an intern, especially working in the communications department. I've always wanted to be this hotshot writer living in Speculo, writing about the trendiest MM products, new and proven weight loss tips, literally everything!" Zasha admits, as if she had been waiting to bust out her life story since laying her crazy eyes on me.

To steer myself from forming some kind of attachment to Zasha too early, my eyes fixate on the silvery platform that Influencer Brecky was standing on. After delicately straightening my charcoal, cable-knit, sweat-proof turtleneck, my tech button projects on the glass wall of Brecky's office. The roomful of interns and Brecky herself respond in furrowed eyebrows and puzzled looks. Letting the echo of my zoomers glide on the floor, my strong calves halt at the platform and begin speaking, as it levitates me upward.

"Hey everyone. It's nice to meet you guys. I was thinking we should really get started on creating some content for the magazine as soon as we can because that's the most important part, right?"

The room adorns itself with nodding heads, and *mhmmm* sounds swarm the room. Wow, who knew they would actually listen to me?

"Listen, I know this might not have been your first choice of placement, but we are all here now together. You guys over there, start writing brief outlines on which high point and low point Speculo residents we could interview. And you two, list out potential feature stories that compare the differences and similarities of those who are at their perfect midpoint versus those who are not. Finally, Zasha! Would you be able to brainsketch some ideas for the magazine layout and graphics?

The phrases, "Who? Me?" and "You got it! What was your name? Ropash...Ropa...Ropashna?" swarm the room.

As I turn around and cascade off the platform, Brecky's platinum blonde hair sashays across her gaping smile, clapping her child-like, daisy-designed talons. "Impressive" she mouths from the barrier. Her pointer finger motions for me to leave Zasha and the rest of the interns to the duties I didn't know would actually manifest.

"Wow, taking leadership already?" Brecky says, swiveling around in her mirror foam office chair. The molding of her peach bum sinking her into the chair makes her look shorter than she actually is.

"I'm just trying my best. Gotta prove that Jeenz invested in me for a reason, even though I don't look like the um... traditional looking Mirror Mania intern," I respond.

Brecky bashfully smiles to the side, licking her baby pink, pillowy soft lips. I wonder if there's more to this Barbie doll. After all, she does have glasses and says "uh," so she can't be *that* dumb, but that might just be some persona she's trying to curate to keep up with Facegram.

"Hm. It looks like you're doing well! Tell me more about you, *Ropashna*," Influencer Brecky says with what I detect as a telling combination of personal curiosity and reporting intrigue.

"Well, you'll know more about me over time. I'm just a hardworking girl and when I want something, I always get it. I have an older brother named Shojan. I love triple chocolate cake with white chocolate frosting, milk chocolate base, and dark chocolate chips. My favorite color is grey because it combines every color. Um... I could go on, but I would have to pause and think about the most interesting of interesting facts about me," I say with a quick and painless body fat caliper pinch of sincerity.

"Cool! We love to see it! Uh uh...I like it! I'm glad you're one of my interns. It's, uh, the first day and you're already taking initiative, so good for you! Just remember I want the, uh, colors to be Mirror Mania specific: red, black, and white.

Classy As Alwayssss!" Brecky bounces out of her chair, transforming her static state into warp speed jumping jacks.

Zero arm jiggle at all.

"Burn Break. Time To Get Your Ass Up And Werk Werk Werk Werk Werk Werk," a metallic voice screech from Brecky's hot pink tech button.

Only Influencers can manage to tattoo the wrist skin bulge of their tech buttons.

Zooming back to my desk, Zasha's brainsketching screeches. The thing about brainsketching is that everyone does it so differently, so uniquely, but she seems the most suited for this because of her creative energy.

Adjusting the black, blocky buttons on the brainband and a crinkled forehead laced with sparkles of sweat, Zasha throws her head around and keeps sketching exactly what she's envisioning.

"This thing is so confusing! I'm so used to tablets and droid scanners!" She complains.

"You can do it. I see that you've drawn some decent graphics already! The swirling staircase letters and chromatic, reflective material are really interesting. I also love the solid red lining of the cover design sketch. How'd you know that we have to stick to classic Mirror Mania colors?" I say, trying to sound professional, instead of keening out of personal interest.

"OOH THANKS, GIRL. That means a lot! This is so difficult. I know because, like I told you, I've always wanted to be a writer at a magazine. Mirror Mania is the biggest one, so I've studied it so much! I've literally read every issue since I was five-point-five years old!" Zasha says with a little too much enthusiasm.

"What... why five-point-five years old? Do you mean five and a half?" I ask.

It still technically qualifies as professional inquiry.

"Oh! I had a teeensy brain injury when it was my half birthday! I like my half birthday better than my actual birthday because it's in the summer, so my family celebrates that as if it's my real birthday. But, yeah! I fell down while we were all playing a game of zoom tag and someone zoomed into me way too fast, crashing my big head to the ground, and the last thing I saw was the latest issue of MM. I woke up two days later and the only thing I could remember was that magazine cover. I still remember what it looked like! It was so pretty, actually. This beautiful, green-eyed beauty with pin-straight black hair being promoted for maintaining her perfect midpoint weight for twenty years straight with absolutely no faltering days. Like ever," Zasha rambles, letting her own eyes glaze over.

"Ah. So, what happened when you woke up?" I say in attempt to cover my third yawn.

Shaking her head and big bug eyes into focus, she says, "Well, I just remember the game and then seeing that Mirror Mania Magazine cover. Nothing else. I thought of it as... like a sign that I lived because I was meant to be part of this magazine and that I have my fair share to contribute to it."

Her black rope necklace and mismatching zoomers make her seem clumsy, yet simultaneously fearless, for not caring about her image so much. Maybe not clumsy, but brilliant in the most unusual way.

"That's pretty awesome," I say, letting half of my mouth curve upward. Who knew that someone so loyal to Mirror Mania would make me *smile*?

Needing a bit of a thinking break, I sink into the mirror doors like chromatic liquid and head to the second floor. Mirror Mania looks pretty from here. The high, open ceilings that let only the lowest heat and UV level rays of sunshine in, the organically grown, hemp booty-growing taste tester dispensers, perfect Facegram capture-worthy families walking around and weighing themselves repeatedly, and white coats of mainly women tapping around in stilettos stained in a sugar-free salsa red. So *pretty*. I remember this used to be what I wanted. Peering at myself at one of the mirror pillars my arms are hugged around, my fingers lace around a strand of my softly curled mane. I notice the little bumps on my forehead. I notice the hair on my skin, but also its smooth suppleness.

"Mirror Mirror on the pole, why do I have such a nasty mole?" A raspy, but feminine voice behind me says, startling me.

A duo of slanted green eyes and almond-shaped hazel eyes with a shivering concoction of chuckling and giggling interrupts my reflection.

"Ah, hello Influencer Jeenz. Hello....hello," I say, immediately clearing my throat and curving my back.

"How is everything going Ropashna? I am sure you are adjusting well," Jeenz intriguingly says as she gracefully dances her lean, yellowy legs around me.

Hazel Eyes stands there, hands cushioned inside his super sexy and thigh-muscle-defining skinpants.

"Poof, boof," his full lips blow unamused puffs of air as an alternate source of amusement. My tongue glides over my lips, but purse as soon as Hazel Eyes breaks his trance.

Jeenz pauses her dance. My nose crinkles out of concentration.

"Oh... uh yes, Jeenz. They've been going well. I've met a few more people, I've already taken in charge of some projects for the magazine and have started to build a relationship with Brecky," I say as if I'm reporting like my life depends on it because it kind of does.

I have to prove some sense of loyalty, so nobody senses my disloyalty. I just don't know why Influencer Jeenz seems to be so interested in me.

"Well, that's superb! Brecky sent me a message on Face-gram about her updates, so I actually already knew all of that. I'm proud of this extremely quick, yet fantastically pleasing progress. I'm looking forward to seeing what more you have in store, Ropashna," Influencer Jeenz squints her eyes and abruptly spins on her chromatic bottomed heel.

Hazel Eyes casually stands there.

"I think your mole is cute by the way," he shyly lets out, making another annoying blowing sound.

"Oh, I don't even know who said that," I shortly respond, waiting for him to bring up what happened at Intern Orientation.

Miss Chubs. God, that situation *still* annoys me. I'm getting annoyed just thinking about it.

"Why were you with Influencer Jeenz anyway?" I try to change the subject.

"Oh, uh. She was impressed with how well I did at Orientation and just wanted to talk."

Just talk? Why does Influencer Jeenz act so uninterested and then she wants to know all of our business?

Hazel Eyes slowly pushes his flat, hard chest to me. The air transforms into a fresh flash-frozen mint. I know it's you, the boy who just wants to make me feel desired just because it's fun to tease *Miss Chubs*.

"Look. I owe you an apology," he quietly lets out. "I didn't mean to be such an asshole. I realize that you were just joking. It really messed with me because I used to be on the bigger side myself until recently, actually, and lots of people made fun of me in my past," he elaborates.

"Huh! I don't believe the perfectly cooked and put-together cocky guy has ever had to go through what I've had to," I tweet back.

"You think I'm perfectly cooked? That's cute, aha. Anyways, you'd be surprised. Most of the times, it's the people you don't think have suffered that are the one who have suffered the most."

"Alright, deep guy. Did you get that off of Facegram?" I half sarcastically ask.

We stand in silence for a bit. I feel a little hesitant to forgive him because I just don't want to get hurt again. What's the point in trusting him if I'm supposed to remain unattached to this place? Even with Zasha, it's *hard*.

"I forgive you only if you finally give me your name," I finally say.

"Only if we can be friends," he conditions back. He accepts my rolling eyes, but contradictory head nod, as a deal.

"Deslin is the name. You were definitely dying to know," the words escape from his intoxicatingly juicy lips that rise into an equally intoxicatingly charming smile.

This whole unattached, stick-to-the-objective, anarchy plan is going to be a lot harder than I thought.

CHAPTER 6

THE BEAUTY BIO SPACE: DESLIN

———

My dad used to always talk about the Beauty Bio Space like it was this special wonderland, gleaming with his favorite toys and blow up dolls. I feel both disgusted and intrigued to be here, especially because I'm used to just being the listener of his experiences.

"Man, people are starting to become more aware of Mirror Mania. Capitalism, ya know?" Jrelito turns to me, scratching his red curls as if he could potentially find the answer in there.

"I mean, yeah. People think there's something wrong with them and Mirror Mania provides the answers. It's just a loop to keep them coming back," I say.

"Well, couldn't you say that people are just trying to improve themselves? Maybe, they just want to be better," Jrelito intriguingly responds.

"Hm. I guess I never saw it that way," I say in a way to maintain the moderate temperature of the conversation before it goes any further.

"Well, it's a mindset, right? Mirror Mania is just an entity, yet it affects so many people in so many different ways," Jrelito says, while his pining eyes forage his tech button projection screen in search of fat-melting chocolate snacks, because only in Speculo do people eat to starve.

His hair mopes in front of him, but he's too infatuated with his work to notice.

"Speaking of bettering yourself... Deslin, you should check this out, bro! I feel like I'm really getting somewhere with th-" Jrelito enthusiastically bursts, but is halted by a slender figure framed by a potent scent of what seems to be eight-year-old electroflowers peering over us.

"With what?" Influencer Jeenz asks with her beautiful face, deadpan and straight.

"Oh... I mean I can work on whatever else we're supposed to be assigned first and then this...project," Jrelito clears his throat, immediately running his hands through his curls, exposing a yellowish face with bushy, but shapely, eyebrows.

"Hi, Influencer Jeenz. We're actually examining some formulas to make fat-melting chocolate bites," I straightforwardly spill.

Jrelito makes his "Bro, what?" face while shaking his head as slow as his comprehension can be at times. I shrug.

"Not horrible, honestly. However, yes. This can wait. I have an announcement for all of you interns, actually." Jeenz blandly says, making her way to a bright crimson bodychair.

Gently squishing herself into the chrome seat, her thin fingers presses the height maximizer. "Swoosh!" The rest of the interns immediately laser their eyes on the now floating Influencer Jeenz, elegantly perched in her molded bodychair, highlighting her godly crafted proportions.

"Yo!" Jrelito whispers and crunches me in the side. I wince.

"You got a little crush already? Thought it would be an intern, bro!" he says with a little too much enthusiasm this time.

I roll my eyes and make a, "Bro, what?" face back.

"Sometimes, your own medicine tastes best, huh?" he adds. We chuckle.

"Listen up, everyone! Congratulations on being part of the most *integral* section of Mirror Mania. This is where all the hard work is done. Mirror Mania relies on the Beauty Bio Space for the present *and* the future," Influencer Jeenz says with a strong, yet seemingly unaggressive tone.

"Every day, we make the most famous products, products that aren't even available for the rest of Speculo City to see!" Jeenz awkwardly exclaims with inflection that questions if she is actually excited.

"I wonder what we'll be making today, *heh*," Jrelito says, twiddling his fingers and tapping his shiny gold zoomers.

What kind of weirdo wears *gold* zoomers?

"Now, since we make products every day, you will need to complete a daily task. All of you interns will be working *together*. I will be watching you all very closely. You will be graded on this," Influencer Jeenz instructs, her powerful echo rumbling the flasks and test tubes.

"What's the task?" I ask.

Her emerald eyes narrow down at me for a split second, but immediately circles her attention to the whole room again.

"Ah, of course. We will be working on Macronutrient Profiling today. We will be adjusting macro ratios in the popular junk food Cheezbits so that we can sell what the people of Speculo crave, especially our 'above maximum pointers,' without sacrificing our greatest priority of health," Influencer Jeenz explains.

Phrases of "Oh damn! I've always dreamt of eating brownies to lose weight!" "We really be making history ova here," and "Let's do it!" pop around the room.

"Oh damn bro! I've always dreamt of eating brownies to lose weight. We really be making history ova here, huh? Let's do it!" Jrelito repeats back, almost out of breath.

Influencer Jeenz is beautiful to look at it, but something about her seems greatly intimidating.

"The current product of Cheezbits carried in most pop-up stores can be found in the supply closet right behind my office. Remember that only Beauty Bio Space members and Influencers have access to this closet," Influencer Jeenz directs with a tone as if she was already losing patience from thinking about having to repeat herself.

Influencer Jeenz nods her shiny white hair, quietly curving her rosy lips to herself. The chair slowly blinks back to the ground, notifying the interns to return back to gazing at their workstations.

"One last thing. You will be needing more protein. Macronutrients can be found in the supply closet as well. We tend to steer away from animal protein, so a lot of our jars are filled with collagen and hemp," Jeenz says.

Jeenz nods her shiny white hair, quietly curving her rosy lips to herself. The chair slowly blinks back to the ground, notifying the interns to gaze back at their work instead.

"How does everyone know what to do already?" Jrelito asks me.

"The Beauty Bio Space isn't for the interns that don't know what they're doing, but your secret is safe with me if you go to the supply closet to grab us a bag of Cheezbits," I joke.

"Not bad! Thought you were too serious to poke at me, bro," he says with raised eyebrows.

Scrambling, veiny hands in water gloves reach for old waxy bags of Cheezbits, determined eyes scan single Cheezbits with their tech buttons, and craned necks extract precise measurements with zaptools all around the room. We're all working together, yet alone in our heads, mainly to impress Influencer Jeenz. Influencer Jeenz slowly steps each pointed black heel with just the right amount of pressure to not make a clacking sound, while observing each intern with the same amount of finesse.

"Secured the bags!"

Jrelito clashes ten bags on our lab zone.

"This seems to be nine more than I asked for. Was the supply closet heaven?" I ask.

"I mean I figured we'd mess up a shit ton and it was alright. You gotta check it out for yourself," he says, nonchalantly shrugging.

At least now I know this dude won't be getting in my way anytime soon.

I rip the bag open, sunshine-yellow Cheezbits scattering themselves on the glass table, begging to be modified. My tech button immediately scans one notoriously yellow bit. "Result: 40 percent carb, 50 percent fat, 10 percent protein," it mechanically reads syllable by syllable.

"We gotta makes sure the macros all imitate the macros to achieve an average perfect midpoint weight for all Speculo City residents, right? 30C, 40F, 30P?" Jrelito asks.

Damn. Maybe he's not as dumb as he lets off.

"Huh, I guess you do know what you're doing. But, yeah. We can use the jars in the macro supply closet since these babes are low on protein," I say.

"Cheezbabes," Jrelito says, with an obnoxious laugh resembling the cracking of Cheezbits in the room.

Scanning into the supply closet, clear jars and gobs of different macronutrients neatly line the gigantic storage space. After picking out prime-grade freeze-dried collagen, the zaptool adjusts the fat and carb amounts and substitutes more protein in to get the perfect ratio in a single Cheezbit. My tech button beeps, saving the Nutrient Profile.

"Damn. You're already at the duplication stage?" Jrelito peers over my side of the lab table.

"Yup. We don't have to waste any Cheezbits because we can take the junky ones and use the saved Profile data on my tech button to scan and zap the rest of the bits in bulk," I explain.

Everyone goes back to quietly working, with interns sporadically yelling out, "Ouch! I just zapped myself!"

They continue meticulously zapping each individual Cheezbit with more concentration and less stamina than the one before. How *dumb* do they have to be to do that?

"So! Will your tech button be able to organize the grams from each macronutrient?" Jrelito ponders with his crystal-like eyes.

"Of course. These grams will be specific for the carb, fat, and protein ratios. I'll just scan over all the Cheezbits bags we have and however many grams of collagen we need for my tech button to collect all of the data," I explain.

With big eyes and a shining smile, Jrelito vigorously wags his head, as if I just approved his formulas for his fat-melting chocolate bites.

"Looking at all this food has me hungry myself, so I'm gonna just get a quick snack from the Motivation Room," I say, but Jrelito's laser goggles blind him from seeing me leave.

As I walk out, I hear Influencer Jeenz's tiny fingernails tap away on her Facegram screen, swiping reviews and products away as if they were mini protein crisp crumbs on stainless mirror counters. I bet everything she uses is made of mirrors. "Already quitting?" she says, not bothering to look up from her sport of swiping.

"Quitting unhealthiness, of course," I say.

She smiles, yet still refuses to identify with my eyes. Making my way past her, my body blends into the large, mirror doors. I haven't been to the Motivation Room on the second floor near the Body Imaging Centre yet. Emerging from the doors into the room, I'm greeted with the backside of Ropashna's gorgeous body. Somehow, I'm distracted by the attention of a chromebot polishing the mirrors with careful grace, as if they were the most cherished texture coded in his microchip.

"How is this place motivating? I just feel even worse about myself and I work here!" Ropashna turns toward me, tucking a stringy piece of her black hair behind her elfish ears.

Her deep brown eyes waver around the rectangular shaped room, examining a digitally projected poster on lowest weight, midpoint weight, and highest weight requirements for different heights and ages of women.

"How can someone survive off of being five-two and 110 pounds for the rest of their life? That's literally insane. What happens when you get pregnant? What if you're naturally curvy? You literally fluctuate pounds every day! Everyone thinks this is what healthy is! This is insane," she rambles on.

Hm, she's kind of cute when she's annoyed about Mirror Mania.

"Well, some people are just skinny," I say, halfheartedly attempting to further provoke her.

She shoots me a face that resembles a crinkled diabetic-friendly protein powder dusted donut left in the freeze drier for too long.

"You try surviving off of being the same weight every day for even just a year then," Ropashna retorts with a raised, defined eyebrow.

"Look, that poster says, 'lose weight so you can finally be happy with yourself!' and that one over there says, 'sink down to a negative clothing size when you try the 80/20 vegan ice cream diet!' They seem pretty motivating to me," I dig back, gesturing all over the room.

"When are we ever going to have a normal conversation?" She turns to me, shaking her head full of sarcasm and sincerity.

A sign to take a chance?

"Well, how about we have a proper conversation at the Annual Sacrifice Masquerade Ball?" I ask her.

Her brown, wondrous eyes constantly shift from left to right as she processes my proposition.

"Hm. I suppose I can meet you there," she sassily says.

"Ah, did you think I was asking you out on a date?" I ask, slyly trying cover up my intentions.

"Not think, just know," Ropashna grins.

I charmingly return the expression.

"I suppose you'll meet me there then?" I suggest.

Suddenly, the sound of glass shattering prevents an answer to my question. Ropashna's eyes widen as a message on her tech button unexpectedly appears on her projected screen. *From Brecky,* my most likely unwanted peering eyes read.

"It was nice not having a normal conversation. I need to get back to work," she promptly says with a mask of seriousness that didn't seem to exist a few seconds before.

"See you at the Masq-" her speedy absence stops me from continuing.

Does she want me to chase her? I shake my head, trying to shed my thoughts. No. Remember why I'm here.

Sinking back into the Beauty Bio Space without accomplishing my original intention of getting a snack, I see Jrelito has finished converting all of the Cheezbits bags that he had managed to hoard at our workspace. Leaning back in his body chair that now resembles more of a bean bag most likely because Jrelito appreciates novelty in all forms, he rummages his fingers through his red nest of curls.

"Dude, how long does it take for you to replenish on motivation?" Jrelito asks.

"I was gone for ten minutes, chill. Good thing you finished everything," I say.

He crosses his light mustard tinted arms, but shrugs.

"To be honest, it was kind of fun, extracting all these tiny little bits that were once seen as cancerous. And now Speculo will praise Cheezbits like they're some kind of magical health food that promises ultimate body perfection for the rest of your life," he says with rolling eyes.

"Right. You ready for that annual masquerade thing?" I ask, tilting my elbows on our lab station.

"Mehhh. I mean the girls are gonna look bangin'. Besides that, it's just another gaudy party for Influencers to talk about themselves. I did hear that it's apparently the biggest event of the year, so maybe it ain't gonna be too bad," Jrelito tiredly says, slowly opening his mouth and expanding his arms back in a Y-shape.

The other interns maintain their focus on the Cheezbits, some still struggling to get through their first bag. Cheezbit dust and pieces crunch from anxiously shaking feet.

"Sleeping or working?" Influencer Jeenz says, seeming to appear out of nowhere.

"Weren't you just on the other side working with them two blonde chicks?" Jrelito asks, squinting his curious emerald eyes.

"Yes, and now I'm here. Status?" Jeenz says directly at me as if Jrelito was a mere fan of hers itching for approval.

"Ah... uh... well we finished about twelve bags," I say, while Jrelito curls his lips and raises another eyebrow at the word "we."

"Not too bad, especially for the time being. Family size, I presume?" she asks. Sticking out a long, somewhat orangey tongue and with expanded eyes, Jrelito speaks without making a sound. He mouths "Ro-bot" behind the side of Influencer Jeenz's muscularly intact back, which is made very much apparent by a crop top with only a string down the middle to highlight her tailbone.

Well, I guess that's one way to *influence*.

Ignoring Jrelito's taunts, I say, "Of course. Did you expect anything less?"

"I honestly expected a bit more, especially from you. I see you wanting to make your place here, you know," she says without a singular twitch in her face.

"I'll make my place," I assert, but quickly loosen my stance.

Influencer Jeenz smiles or at least slightly upturns her lips and nods her head. Still refraining from giving Jrelito any recognition, she seamlessly glides back to her office.

The "two blonde chicks," in Jrelito's words, turn their heads as far as they can go to tactfully scan the specific design and pattern of Influencer Jeenz's yellow zoomers. Their whispers and giggles disrupt some of the other working interns.

"What do you think those two are gossiping about?" Jrelito leans over to me.

"Probably how much Jeenz weighs or how she has it so easy since she's always at her perfect midpoint weight or something," I say.

"How much do you think she weighs?" Jrelito asks.

My face scrunches.

"Well, she's an Influencer, so not much. I bet she doesn't have many problems other than dissuading her stalkers or deciding which vegetable is fresher to eat. She's around five-six, so I would say..." my fingers move to my chin and I look up at the transition ceiling, realizing one of the interns must have changed the background to sugar-free candyland.

Jrelito flashes on his inspecting, beady eyes again.

"Dude. It's not that deep. The lady is probably like 130 pounds. That seems about right. Then again, I don't really know shit about all this weight stuff, man. I've never really worried about it too much," he says.

"Ah, must be nice," I say, purposely holding myself back.

"Bro, we're probably the same. Actually, what have you had to worry about? Look at those damn biceps, bro!" His unusually beefy and clammy fingers make a cupping motion around my upper arms, squeezing me like a personal plush toy.

"Yeah, I mean. I didn't always look like this," I say with a chuckle.

"Ah, one of them beefy bois when you were a kid, huh," he says, jabbing his thick finger into my abs.

"I wouldn't be talking," I say.

"Ay! Whatchu sayin'?" Jrelito loudly defends himself while his hands lift up his loose, red shirt to expose his own set of defined abs.

My tech button beeps before Jrelito and I can finish prodding each other about deep-rooted issues from my childhood.

"What's that? That little Ropa girl? The one with the dark hair and big booty?" Jrelito pokes.

"You jealous?" I say back. Too tired to keep sparring, Jrelito sighs into his molded chair, positioning his feet up on the glass, and shuts his eyes as fast as I want to text Ropashna back.

Suddenly I'm not so tired as my eyes read her message.

"Yes."

"Yes. To what?" I respond.

"I thought you were smart, or not dumb, at least. Anyway, I am saying yes as a response to your question on meeting you at the Annual Masquerade."

CHAPTER 7

THE SACRIFICE MASQUERADE BALL: ROPASHNA

———

Slowly extending my right arm to reach my navy-blue silk sheets that are crumpled on the floor, I examine my open window. There's a tiny frail man with a booming voice and nails that seem to be digging straight into his wrist. Slick Bullets pass by him slowly and turn on their body scanners; they're probably all competing to see who can send information to Mirror Mania the fastest.

Huh. I bet if Influencer Anastasia or any other Influencer were screaming outside, it would be trendy instead of threatening.

My wavy hair scatters across my drool-stained pillow, as I plop back on my bed and reflect on how long it's been since Intern Orientation. Everything is surprisingly going accordingly in the Communications and Analytics Department. No one seems to suspect anything.

I've become closer with Zasha naturally, like I didn't even have to try. It's interesting how minorities always attract one another out of comfort, but then the rest of the world complains we're teaming up against them. We've been getting frozen egg white shakes from Mirror Mania Munch, a gaudy café that serves snack-sized portions of what feels like hefty bites of air entering your stomach. I usually leave hungrier than I came. Today, it's the day of Mirror Mania's *Annual Sacrifice Masquerade Ball*. Zasha and I have been talking about it every day now. For the rest of Speculo City, it's the day of Sacrifice.

"Hey, Rat. I heard there's that dance thing tonight. You going?" My brother Shojan peers by my room doorway.

"Yeah. I can't wait to see if there are any cute guys, ones that like to call me Miss Chubs!" I say.

He laughs, but shakes his egg-shaped head disapprovingly, while perching himself near the glittery, gold-painted wood edge of my bed.

"You know I always tell you to speak kindly to yourself. Remove Deslin from your thoughts. He's not even in the Communications and Analytics Department."

"When you say it, it sounds so obvious and easy," my words mumble out of me echoed by a few awkward laughs.

"I know that it's not, so that's why I try to say it that way. That way, you don't go all Rampage Ropa on me," Shojan gently comments with a half-smile.

I've always admired that about him. He knows what to say to calm me down. My eyes flutter to the ground. He has a point. I keep wanting more attention even after my conversation with Deslin, but I barely know him, so why is it affecting my self-worth so much? Quickly checking my tech button, I realize that it's 1:00 p.m.

I jump out of my bed and fumble around the pile of clothes inside my walk-in closet that I wish could have been two times bigger.

"Ropa, I hope you have fun tonight. Mom and Dad are kind of bummed you won't be there tonight since we always celebrate Sacrifice together. Every year since you were a child, you've stayed up with the family to watch the Sacrifice ceremony," Shojan continues.

Sacrifice is celebrated all over the city, but only Mirror Mania and special invite guests attend the *Sacrifice Masquerade Ball*. During Sacrifice, a residence of Speculo is nominated for being too above or below their midpoint. Back when it all started, the nominee used to actually be sacrificed and used for god knows what, but now it's just to keep up tradition and an excuse to party. I'm the very first one in my family to attend the ball, but I still don't know why. That's why I have to talk to Influencer Jeenz *tonight*. I just want to know why a girl 20 pounds over her maximum point with no family ties to Mirror Mania was accepted.

Distractedly, I look back at Shojan, and notice a faint scar in the shape of a five-pointed star on his wrist.

"I know. It kind of sucks. I was thinking about if I should really go or if I should stay," I say, squinting at the scar, appearing darker the more I stare.

"Go. It'll be fun! We'll always be here," he encourages.

My tech button shoots out a projection of all my apps, but a large red notification box interrupts the organized scenery: "new messages from Zasha."

I refocus my attention on Shojan.

"Sorry, I'm just getting ready now. But yeah. You're right," I say.

"Of course I am. I always am," he grins.

Shojan shifts around, stretching his lanky body up, while I patch on some sparkly silver liquid eyeliner.

"Why is there a scar on your wrist, Shoju?" I decide to pry, tilting my head back.

"Bruh, that's been there forever. C'mon, Ropa. You spend all your time at Mirror Mania, and you forget about scars I've had since I was born?" he responds a bit more defensive than usual.

"Oh! That was from your tech button surgery, right?" I ask.

"Yup. Some Beauty Bio Space Influencer messed up when she was inserting the electronic chip in my wrist, so instead of a regular button shape, it's like a star. She didn't even make the proper incisions, so I have some scarring that reoccurs every now and then," he explains.

"I bet you were crying and wailing everywhere," I lightly tease.

"I was a baby!" he defends himself.

Everyone in Speculo City is required to have a tech button. Some of my old tech button apps locked me out because I have to be under my maximum point to use them. They were my favorites too! There's Fashion Modeling, where clothes are tried on virtually. There's also World Tasting, which is feeling sensations of eating different cuisines around the world without even having to physically move a single inch. I *really* miss them.

"Alright. I'm gonna let you do whatever this all is," Shojan says, waving his hands in a rounded motion toward my half-applied eyeliner and rummaged clothes.

"Ha. Ha," I say with a twisted face and tongue poking out of my somewhat chapped lips.

A pair of gigantic, unblinking, purple eyes and whispy blonde strands pop up on my wall.

"Heeyy girl! What are you wearing tonight? Scandalous and sexy or classy and cute?" Zasha's clear skin seems to say, except a mini array of forehead zits.

"Um, how about neither because you know I don't like *exclusive* categories. Like, why do I have to be considered scandalous if I'm dressed sexy and not considered cute, or both at the same time?" I question.

"You always kill the vibe! Well, I'm wearing a traditional skirt and handmade crop top from Sunare. It's beaded with orange jewels and tons of sequins and the cloth is satin. To *absolutely* die for! Don't you think?" she squeals in excitement, her blonde streaks whipping around her heart-shaped face.

"Zasha, it's great. I'll see you tonight. Remember to come over at six, so we can take a bullet together!" I say, shuddering a little bit after realizing I sound like Mom.

Her face already disappears.

I don't usually like telling people what I'm going to wear because I love to surprise them. I strip off my purple kitten pajamas and hop in the shower. The water refreshingly coats my parched skin and the steamy air smells like a mix of Mom's hot Sezolun chili chicken from the open crack of my room door and whatever fruity-scented soap that Dad thinks I like.

I get out and prepare a bath with Hair Begone. The white liquid instantly dissolves as I dunk my body in, while grimacing a bit, but step out two minutes later with a completely hairless body.

"Ropaaa! Come eat a snack before you go!" Mom endearingly yells, not sounding as annoying as usual.

I hitch up my dress and gingerly take balanced steps out of my room, relying all of my weight and first impression onto our spiral staircase railings.

"Mom, I'm already looking so bloated. Do you want me to look even worse?" I say from the top of the staircase.

Standing below, she gives me a look that kills me and says, "No. No. I just wish you were coming tonight. You know it's family tradition for us to gather on Sacrifice. You look nice. I love the dress. That's the one I brought for you, hm?"

"Yes! I love the lavender and white lace detail," I excitedly say, letting her know that her purchase was worth it.

I feel a pang of nostalgia hit me at once. Suddenly, I miss the tradition of playing board games with my cousins and watching my mom cook three hundred Sezolun dishes only to be devoured within minutes. Slowly thumping up the stairs, Dad peaks out to see me off.

"Leaving now? Have fun, pretty girl," he sloppily kisses my forehead, leaving a similar glistening residue after completing an intense body weight burn workout.

The doorbell blares. Mom rushes to the door before I can leave without having to introduce Zasha.

"You look stunning!" Zasha says with too much enthusiasm that I doubt her sincerity.

Heat disperses throughout my face. For some reason, when it's family complimenting me it doesn't feel as awkward.

"See you guys!" Mom, Dad, and Shojan squawk in unison, waving their hands.

Zasha and I get into our Bullet that drops us off at the glowing entrance of Mirror Mania with people dressed in all types of graceful gowns, sparkly heels, face-covered feather hats, arms decorated with boyfriends, wives, and other confidence boosters. Zasha and I put on our masks.

"I love masquerades. There's such charm about hiding who you are for a bit," I say to Zasha, not really wanting to hear her thoughts.

"Why would you ever want to hide who you are?" she says with a face dripping of innocent optimism.

I sigh. Sometimes, I forget she's probably like 120 pounds and doesn't have to worry about much.

"Oh shit! There are two droid guards checking everyone's body weight!" Zasha nudges me but doesn't seem to assume I might get stopped.

Who is this girl? Can she really be this genuine?

"Pass." The droid succinctly lifts its heavy white arms to let me join Zasha inside.

I'm so confused how I can get through all this security.

The lobby looks nothing like how it usually does. It's packed with people, droids, hologram pets, and fountains of zero-calorie alcohol. I overhear some conversations.

"Oh, Charlotte! I'm on the Fuck Real Food diet. It's absolutely marvelous. Who knew that I would be able to have such stellar results by starving myself of delicious starches, fruits, and even nutrient-dense vegetables! My hair is falling off and I'm cold all of the time!" The lady begins to cry, and who I assume is Charlotte comforts her, while secretly being happy that she hasn't lost her own willpower yet.

I've sworn to never diet again after being just as obsessed and overwhelmed as most of the women here.

"Ropashna! Should we meet up with the other interns?" Zasha asks like a child begging for a midpoint friendly dessert.

"Yeah, let's do it." I nonchalantly respond.

I agree because it's not like any of them will recognize me with my mask on, unless they look at my ass. We walk to the corner of other interns. Most girls are dressed pretty slutty, but one wears an ankle-length, form-fitted, amethyst-colored dress. The guys wear navy blue suits that they probably bought for a cousin's wedding at some point in the last three years.

While socially distracted Zasha chats away, I decide to try and hunt down Influencer Jeenz. A few figures in a dim lit corner disappear into the mirror doors. I follow them inside to the Beauty Bio Space, which is transformed into a gallery filled with all kinds of leisure and celebratory activities.

"It's all so amazing, isn't it?" a husky voice says a little too close to my ears, but I don't mind. I recognize that voice, but don't feel like turning around.

My eyes fixate on a floating table of different cuisines, including Sezolun! My eyes gape at the work of art tower designed from high-protein cupcakes, sugar-free donuts, and vitamin cake pops: classic Mirror Mania finger foods. On the other side, Beauty Bio Space vendors with Influencers testing new products for weight loss solutions crowd the area.

"It's more than that. It's an illusion, and one that is so enticing that it's hard to see it's a trap," I say.

"But isn't that the purpose of an illusion?" Deslin says, spinning in front of me.

The chatter in the room simmers, redirecting the attention to a big, blue-haired woman with features that resemble a peacock: piercing blue almond-shaped eyes, nose piece glasses with a blue shiny beaded chain connected to a long and crooked nose.

"Welcome everyone! Thank you for coming to the Annual Sacrifice Masquerade Ball. Let's get started right away with the sacrifice, so we can all enjoy our time and waste the rest of the night together! Who's ready?" Peacock Lady squeals in admirable delight.

The room roars. The people at the tables next to me are dressed in white, sparkling gowns and perfectly ironed tuxedos, yet accessorized with blank facial expressions. I observe them as they mindlessly clap like obedient droids.

"The thing about Mirror Mania is that there is no single leader, or at least nobody who's the face of it all. There's been rumors that there *is* a leader, but he or she stays disguised amongst the other influencers," Deslin leans in and whispers in my ear.

His fresh, smooth breath relaxes me from staring at Peacock Lady's loud appearance. Looking around, my eyes lock with Influencer Anastasia and Influencer Brecky. Influencer Brecky nods and shyly pokes her glasses, while Influencer Anastasia rolls her unsuitable boring grey colored contact eyes.

"Well then, I guess I'm going to find him or her," I say with determination.

Deslin just looks at me and squints, seeming like he wants to say something, but stops himself.

"You know, I can't believe I'm actually watching the sacrifice in person, and not on my memory foam sofa at home," he says to change the topic.

"Don't you just feel suffocated with all that memory foam?" I ask.

"Nah. That's the point." He chuckles.

I feel queasy. I've never really liked the ceremony. Even though nobody actually gets sacrificed, it's disgusting to think about.

"Which one of you special invitees are the fattest tonight? Which one of you have been the worst at ignoring the fact that you need to lose weight to get back into your range?" Peacock Lady hollers out to the audience.

The room equally responds in roars again. Heat rushes to my cheeks and my throat is tight. I'm scared that I might hear my name get called. I'm only 20 pounds over my maximum and I will stop at nothing to tear this place apart, yet I'm still fearful and still insecure about that damn number sometimes.

"Well, you know who you are! My dear special guests, did you really think you were invited to further pack on those pounds? There are people starving in Speculo that need your extra weight, don't you think? Let's see. Ekon, Nitin, and Xiu come up on stage! Don't be afraid. Show us that fab flab!" Peacock Lady continues to mock as a form of entertainment.

Two extremely oversized gentleman, one with a scraggly salt-and-pepper beard and the other with a shiny bald head walk up on stage. After, a decently hefty woman with overly chunky arms wobbles on up after him. Everyone cheers. I stare, and the boy who made fun of me for being just like the people on stage that I supposedly forgave creeps his hand onto mine.

"It's going to be alright," Deslin whispers.

Deslin knows. He already knows that I'm not one of them. Ekon, Nitin, and Xiu all look *normal*; they look excited even. They don't seem to be aware of what's happening.

"So, Ekon. You're twenty-four. You're over your maximum by 112 pounds. Xiu, you're twenty-one and over your maximum by 60 pounds. Nitin, you're just sixteen, yet over your maximum by 80 pounds. Congratulations on being the three heaviest people in Speculo!" Peacock lady continues.

The whole room is laughing, screaming, and cheering, including Influencer Anastasia. Influencer Brecky shies her face away, but lightly giggles. I start to wonder where Influencer Jeenz is and if she would be laughing too.

"This is why I weigh myself every day. I don't want to end up like *her*," I overhear from a group of girls next to me chat about Xiu.

The walls of the Beauty Bio Space is encapsulated by Mirror Mania data of the three nominees.

"Vote! Vote for who should be sacrificed to Mirror Mania's Beauty Bio Space! This year, the person sacrificed will be used for fat injections in butt and breast implants," Influencer Anastasia appears on stage to instill more hype.

Deslin's veiny hands still remain clasped with mine.

"I wonder if she's the leader?" I look at him and say.

"Hmm. Maybe. I doubt it," he says slowly with his main focus on taking in everything that's happening.

I clench Deslin's hand deeper, almost digging my sharp nails into his smooth skin.

"The public doesn't even know about this! My family is sitting at home eating and laughing, while this is going on. To think this was one of my favorite holidays growing up," I continue blabbering to Deslin.

He just nods his head and swallows, as if the nominees were projections of himself. Maybe that's why we bond so well.

"I have to go. I can't stand to watch the results. I'm sorry!" I pull my hand away from Deslin, rushing back into the now somewhat empty lobby.

With a blurred vision and a pounding head, my feet stumble me around, but I manage to see a white-colored bob of hair turn around. The body of the bob motions its fingers for me to come forward.

"I've never enjoyed this part either," a feminine, but still assertive voice empathizes.

"Wait. Influencer Jeenz is that you?"

It's difficult to know for sure with her shimmery, lime-green mask covering her equally green eyes.

"You finally have me alone. I've been wanting to talk as well, but I'm busy. What do you want?" she sternly demands yet sounds interested in my presence.

I feel my head pounding even more.

"I really just want to know how and why I was accepted."

"Simple. You're an experiment for change," she says as if there's no more to discuss.

"An... experiment? For what?" I pry.

Cheers and stomping from upstairs in the Beauty Bio Space parade the ambience of the lobby.

"Well, Ropashna. It's no surprise now that Mirror Mania and its, um, practices have become quite toxic. In short, accepting you will be the start to the *new* Mirror Mania," she recites to the point.

"Who's *we*?" I ask.

"Well, *we* take out Influencers. There are others, but you will have to prove if you can be part of this project and our team. Assassination is our latest method. We're done with this regime," she blatantly says, without any twitching of her jade, matted lips.

Assassination? Is that really the way I should be taking down Mirror Mania? Is this a trap?

"Assassination? I mean, I'm all for it, but why do *you* want to help?" I curiously ask.

My head starts twisting and turning with possible scenarios and I can't seem to keep my focus on Influencer Jeenz in front of me.

"Nobody listens to me. I have other Influencers too that feel marginalized, as if what we say doesn't matter. Some Influencers just don't care and use us for experiments. Nobody listens to anyone. There's no sense of unity. I could go on forever," Influencer Jeenz lists off, oddly with no emotion in her face, but her tone evokes otherwise.

Footsteps ponder behind me, stopping next to my position, breaking me out of my dazed confusion.

"So, I guess you did manage to find the leader after all, Ropashna," Deslin pressingly affirms followed by a brief chuckle.

PART TWO

REFLECTIVE

CHAPTER 8

MIRROR MAZE: DESLIN

———

Ropashna's face looks back at me, glowing in surprise and confusion. Meanwhile, Influencer Jeenz stands there with not much of an expression and arms crossed, as if she was already anticipating this moment.

"Wha-what? How do *you* know who the leader is?" Ropashna asks with furrowed brows, pointing one of her short, stubby fingers at me.

"I figured it out at Intern Orientation, actually. Influencer Jeenz would always randomly disappear and seemed quite familiar with Mirror Mania, yet extremely disinterested."

I throw my eyes over at Influencer Jeenz, slowly nodding her head to confirm my story.

"And he just wouldn't leave me alone, so I asked him the same thing I asked you about what you wanted from me. He told me he wanted to destroy Mirror Mania just like you, Ropashna. Ever since then, we have been preparing a plan to get that done." Influencer Jeenz uncrosses her arms.

Ropashna intently stares at a half-eaten gourmet protein brownie on the thick red velvet rug of the lobby floor.

"It would be amazing if you would join us, Ropashna," I say trying to search for a way to maintain her eye contact.

"I've been… I've been wanting to take this place down since the day I applied for the internship," Ropashna finally manages to say.

"Well then, thanks for admitting what we all already know. Let us commence then, shall we? Follow me," Influencer Jeenz dryly says.

While Ropashna and I follow Jeenz to the Beauty Bio Space, Ropashna's lack of giggling tells me that she's still trying to process everything. I knew there was something different about her. I just didn't know it was her being similar to me is what makes her so different. Walking inside, Influencer Jeenz hops onto one of the bean bags in the Beauty corner.

"Alright, Deslin and I have been working on a plan to derail this place, but we have barely made progress," Influencer Jeenz distractedly says while fiddling with her tech button.

Images of targeted Influencers, notes and detailed scribbles are projected on the wall.

"I just don't know what to say," Ropashna barely murmurs, returning her eyes to the floor again.

"I will be blunt with you. We assassinate Influencers. We will *continue* to assassinate them. One by one until this place is changed."

Ropashna's cheeks grow red while her deep chocolate brown eyes casually look around the Beauty Bio Space.

"I want to destroy this place, but is this really the way? It has to be if even Jeenz, the supposed Head of Mirror Mania, feels like there's no other way," Ropashna swiftly turns to me and whispers.

Influencer Jeenz zooms in on the screen with her long, bony pointer finger, displaying a large board of virtual faces. Not gonna lie, they're pretty hot.

"This whole assassination concept is a fairly recent development. We have assassinated two Influencers so far. It is not so much about numbers as it is about the amount of power our targets hold. If we are caught, then we all will be held in detainment to be sacrificed at the next annual Sacrifice Masquerade Ball. I will be discussing more with you at a later date, Ropashna," Influencer Jeenz explains directly at Ropashna with an informational yet compelling tone.

I shiver as I imagine stepping up on that stage, humiliated and feeling like I failed myself.

"So, I will be working on my own management duties. Deslin and Ropashna, you both will be working together as a team. Your first tasks will start off small. Focus on posting on Facegram about practicing Influencing to your followers. The more residents of Speculo that fight back, the stronger our cause becomes. Subtly talk to your fellow interns and see if you can get them to join you," Influencer Jeenz continues to the both of us this time.

She sounds professional when she talks yet looks so young and just like the other Influencers.

"I understand. How do I know I can trust you? How do I know this isn't all just an act?" Ropashna asks.

"You don't and you never will know if you can fully trust me, but that's with all things in life. I'm sure you know this. Just ask Deslin why he was so quick to trust me," Influencer Jeenz dryly says, except with a slight perkiness from the mentioning of my name.

"Ropashna, remember that we both have went through what you have. You can trust us," I glance over, as Ropashna and Influencer Jeenz just observe one another.

The silence is adorned with Ropashna's occasional deep breaths.

"Alright. It sounds solid. I'm still confused with what exactly we are doing, but I want to know everything that is happening at all times. I want to play an integral role in this operation," Ropashna immediately darts her eyes at Influencer Jeenz.

Rushes of excitement, fear, and surprise send tingling sensations all over my body. I have no idea how this girl amazes me, but she also scares me. I feel like I'm threatened by her boldness yet inspired by it all at once.

"Well said. I have a place to destroy. Now go and prove yourselves," Influencer dismisses us with the wave of a dainty hand.

"Well, that was a lot," Ropashna turns to me, as we walk back into the mirror corridor to get to the lobby.

"It was, but I'm glad you agreed to work with us," I say with sincerity.

She looks up at me and smiles with a charming glint in her eyes.

"Deslin, would you like to go to Mirror Maze? That is, if you're not doing anything right now," she abruptly asks.

I'm taken aback by her forwardness, but it's oddly refreshing.

"Sure. That would be nice," I say, trying not to sound overly excited.

Ropashna's tiny feet patter in front of me with her hair sweeping right above her perfect ass. I want to tell her that she looks nice, but somehow a compliment seems like too much of an invitation.

"The streets look *so* empty today, huh?" Ropashna says, as we push open the great mirror doors to the rest of Speculo on an Augleria midafternoon day.

I notice her eyes spot the nearby entrance metallic laced gates of Mirror Maze, one of Speculo City's most popular places to hang out, or I guess go on a date. I mean, this shit better be a date.

"Yeah. Clandell's gloomy weather can be depressing sometimes. I find it hard to even get out of the house when it gets like this," I try to keep up the conversation.

"Definitely! I used to always love gloomy weather back when my whole life revolved on how much I weighed. It was an excuse to not wear shorts or even get out of the house because I was just too insecure," Ropashna lets out.

Why does she act like she trusts me so *easily*?

"Dang. That's rough. When I was a kid, I was basically obese, so I know how it feels to not want to get out of the blanket and feel exposed," I surprisingly reveal back.

It's easy to talk to her. I don't feel so afraid or alone.

"Look! We're here. They have a new ride," Ropashna points to a slide with a bunch of screaming, skinny girls covered in toxin-free chrome. There's more chrome-infused paint splashing on the outsides of the slides, and a blood river with high metabolism guys showing off their abs on floating tubes.

"I love the chrome dip. Mirror Maze has so many cool attractions! There's a big stone rock that I used to jump off of with my old high school friends. We did stupid shit like that because it was fun, but mainly to show off how our tits bounce to the guys," Ropashna keeps talking, feeling free to open herself up.

"Wow. You're so honest," I quietly murmur.

The chrome pool engages most of my attention. I can't have her see me drowning in it and looking stupid.

"C'mon! We have to go jump off the rock! It'll be so fun. I'll go first, I promise," she says with pleading eyes and a soft tone, as if she can tell how scared I am.

I can't resist. Maybe I can do this. I might feel proud when I jump in. Maybe I won't look stupid.

Ropashna clasps my hand. We pass by the silvery splattered steps with the projected screen balloons floating around us: "Welcome to Mirror Maze! Revitalize and Recreate. Developed for recreational and beauty purposes."

Ropashna turns to me. "You got this. Don't be afraid to fall. If we're going to be a team, you have to trust me, anyway."

"You have a point. I'm just so scared of drowning. I'm scared of losing control," I say a little more frightened than I wish.

Suddenly, the wind ferociously whirls around me and Ropashna is nowhere to be found.

"The best moments are when you lose control!" she shouts as she slides down the rock.

I gingerly peer my eyes over. When her head doesn't pop up, my throat begins to clench.

"I'm waiting for you!" she eagerly shouts from below with a bright thumbs up.

Pussy. Are you still that same fat and insecure kid? I bet she only wants to see you jump in to make fun of you. I'm struggling to get over the edge, but Ropashna just keeps cheering me on. Who the hell is this girl? Why does she care so much if I jump?

"Stop thinking! Just let go!" she shouts again.

All of a sudden, I feel like I just smashed my nose up against a mirror. It's just all silver and chrome, and it's surprisingly satisfying. It's like the privilege, and sometimes a burden, of seeing the world no longer matters. My lungs naturally fill themselves with air, as I barely glimpse the bland sky.

"I knew you could do it! You're even kicking too!" Ropashna sashays her chrome-outlined tits over to me.

Our faces gleam with smiles and cheers, splashing chrome dip all over each other. It feels good to let go. I should have been a damn *man* sooner.

"It was definitely hard, but that was honestly... really fun," I say, actually convincing myself.

We get out and flick off the chrome paint with the body scanner washers.

"Nice first date, eh?" I suggestively glance over at Ropashna, noticing how much tighter her pants look from being wet.

"Hmm. It wasn't too bad. Technically, you asked me to the dance!" She engages back.

"Ah, yes. I mean, we did have some time together before you decided to run off," I say with a grin, flipping my charming switch back on.

Shaking her head, a few sparks of chrome fly off.

"I was nervous before with everything but going to Mirror Maze made me feel a lot better," she glances up at me with those dazzling brown eyes again.

"Yeah. Assassinations and all that," I affirm.

She's easy to talk to, but I know we can't talk about *everything*. What's the fun in that?

Her caramel skin glows in the sun and her hair has a dark brownish tinge with just the right amount of light. It's fun noticing these little things about her.

"I had a great time today... and at the dance too. I should really get going. See you soon!" She runs off with her tech button to her ear, exiting the gates to the perfectly timed arrival of a Bullet.

The blaring of my tech button goes off as soon as she gets in and leaves.

"Where are you? I know you're not at Mirror Mania, so don't lie," a strong, deep voice booms on the other end.

"Coming home soon, Dr. Ubili," I try to cover the screaming and laughing around me.

It works and as usual, Dad hangs up without saying bye. The sky swirls with darkness, but I feel the opposite. Though Ropashna and I didn't even go to the actual maze part, I saw all kinds of versions of myself today.

The drones repeat that it's closing time, and the paraded rush of other Speculo residents pours into the available Bullets outside the gates.

"Deslin. Did you gain her trust?" Influencer Jeenz messages me on Facegram.

I forgot this damn thing is connected to literally everyone in Speculo.

"Yes. She's wonderful," I message back.

"Good. Continue as planned," she says.

The warm air around me mixes with gusts of frigid wind.

CHAPTER 9

PHOTO SHOP: ROPASHNA

———

I've actually really liked being a part of the Communications and Analytics Department so far, especially learning about digital marketing and brain advertising by targeting Facegram users through personal data and activity on their tech buttons. It's interesting how most users don't even think about how random ads pop up on their screens. It's as if they're all brainwashed into just waiting for the next Mirror Mania tip or product, so they can finally achieve their perfect midpoint weight.

Zasha interrupts my thoughts as she situates her elbows on my desk, which is scattered with tablets and floating notecards.

"Girrrlll, time flies, doesn't it? I can't believe we've been interning for a few months already. It feels like Orientation was just a few days ago," Zasha says, while noshing on some high-protein collagen gum in between her lips.

Her oddly strong fingers flick my floating notecards back onto the desk.

I drop my pen on my glass workspace and look up.

"I know, but I'm excited we finally get to work on this issue of Mirror Mania's Magazine," I say.

"Ugh. Why do you only care about working and doing the absolute most all of the time? Don't you need a break?" She rolls her eyes while still flicking around the rest of my floating notecards.

"Look, I'm just motivated. I can't take a break because if I do, all I think about is working. We're both minorities, Zasha. We're not the skinniest or the prettiest either, which means I have to work twice, sometimes thrice, as hard as everyone else just to be acknowledged!" I defensively say.

Zasha's voice surprisingly dwindles in energy. She purses her magenta-stained lips.

"So deep all of the time, too."

I laugh and say, "Maybe you should try it sometime."

Her blonde highlighted hair blows out of her face, revealing a sheepish grin.

The Photo Shop corner starts clashing with noise with bright neon-orange-, pink-, and teal-colored blocks tumbling everywhere.

"Hey, Ropashna! Check out our projections. There's this cool story that we covered about a middle-aged guy 30 pounds above his high point," an intern with waxy, lime green, spiky hair howls out, sitting on one of the neon orange squeezechairs.

I get up from my area and zoom over to Mr. Spiky Hair, noticing the chair squeezing and shaping the intern's pale thighs on the selected button image of a thigh gap.

"Alright, this guy named Droland basically details how everyone on the street looks at him like he's homeless. Facegram even refuses to let him find a date to match with! He feels like his life is cursed simply because he's over his high point," Mr. Spiky Hair announces.

"That's great content. We could highlight his quotes, instead of a full feature, unless you have a specific story or experience of his?" I ask, coating my voice with professionalism, as I see Brecky lowering her crimson frames to observe us from the corner of my eye.

"Yeah! Droland has been going to Mirror Maze as a kid, riding the controlled waves on his zoomboard for years. As he got older and gained more weight, he noticed his experiences at Mirror Maze weren't as fun anymore. He used to think it was just age, but he realized it was because of how he looked. When he would get into the chrome dip, the droids would decrease the height and frequency for the waves because they thought Droland would drown and couldn't handle himself," a mousy intern chimes in.

My attention wavers to the distracting, yet intriguing decorations. The Photo Shop corner is drenched in pinned-up before and after photos and heavily edited Influencer profile pictures.

"Also, Droland mentions how some droids would approach him and force him to cover his body with a towel whenever he wasn't in the water. 'It's part of social protocol,' they would tell him," Mr. Spiky Hair further adds on.

Social protocol. Really?

"This is great stuff. I will definitely add this into the magazine. Thank you, guys! Keep covering new stories and getting quotes," I say as motivationally assertive as possible. Brecky and I make eye contact, as I slide back over to Zasha only to see her working soundly at her own cubicle.

I finally have time to start mapping a plan on piecing together the full magazine, more article ideas, and a possible launch party. I wonder if the launch party would be a great time to out all the Influencers and assassinate them.

"Ropashna, good to see you taking charge! Again," Brecky's squeaky voice comments over my hunched shoulders.

"Oh, thanks, haha. I am really enjoying learning what it takes to be at the front of a publication like this," my mouth enthusiastically says, but my head is somewhere else.

Are Influencer Jeenz words really getting to my head? She doesn't even want us to kill that many, just the important ones. It's hard to tell who those people are. Maybe that Dr. Ubili guy? All I want to do is focus on whoever our target is. I need to know this is actually happening.

"Ah, um, cool! You're doing wonderful! Hopefully my weird staring didn't creep you guys out. I know my, um, eyelashes don't look the best today, so I... um, look like a, um, sort of owl creature! Ahah," Brecky nervously says, shifting her weight.

Wow, a blonde and blue-eyed Influencer that's insecure? Now that's a creepy creature I've never encountered before.

"Don't worry, Influencer Brecky. You're gorgeous," I say distractedly.

Influencer Brecky gently smiles and patters her ballerina feet away. Speaking of Influencers, the last time I spoke to Influencer Jeenz in person was the day Deslin and I went to Mirror Maze. Ever since then, I've just been collecting my own notes, observing the department, and slowly talking to other staff and interns about their satisfaction with Mirror Mania.

Deslin and I are a different story. Since we're in separate departments, we usually meet during lunch break in the Motivation Room and message on Facegram. And by meeting during lunch break, I mean breathing heavy and kissing 'til the very last minute before we have to weigh ourselves back in. I mean, it is *definitely* a way to replenish our motivation.

Lately though, I've been feeling like our connection is really growing into more than just hooking up in the

Motivation Room near the Body Imaging Centre. It's hot to see what we look like while we're smashed up against each other, but sometimes I just want to talk or go do actual activities, like when we went to Mirror Maze or the Masquerade together.

Suddenly, the lunch bell clamors through the Communications and Analytics Department. I quickly weight myself out before Zasha can come back to cling herself onto me.

"Hey, you," Deslin approaches me, immediately gripping my waist and pushing me up against a heavy mirror pillar.

He smells like fresh, seven-day-lasting organic pine cologne.

"Hey, there's something I would like to talk to you about, actually," I say with as much confidence as I can.

His gentle, but firm grip around my padded waist makes me feel conflicted if he'll take me seriously with what I'm about to say.

"Of course. What's up?" he nonchalantly says, leaning back on one of the ledges.

"I just, I don't, ugh. Look, I think I have feelings for you. I like you, okay?" I say, while looking at the floor, afraid to see his charming smile replaced with a pitiful one.

Instead, he tilts my chin forward and flashes a sexy, bright grin.

"I've been waiting for you to admit that for a while now, actually," Deslin says.

My heart does not drop. Instead, I'm relieved. Suddenly I have the urge to slap his pretty face, but I can't because of those enchanting hazel eyes.

"So, you like me too?" I shyly question out of reassurance.

"You know I do," he gently says, knowing it would calm me down.

My cheeks rise with warmth and he comes closer to me, but I don't want to rush anything.

"Wait, I think we should take it slow. I know we've been making out and getting closer, but I think I just need more time to get to know you," I let out.

My hand slides against Deslin's rough fingers.

"Girl, we've been talking for a while, but don't worry. There's no pressure," he says with a shrug.

We stand there smiling at one another for a bit, knowing that there's no going back now. I don't want to get distracted. Embraced in each other's arms and with our new little world together, the slight goosebumps on my skin tell me that someone is watching.

A pair of cheetah-printed colored contact eyes sneer at us. Shouldn't *we* be the ones sneering at someone wearing cheetah-printed colored contacts?

"Interns. What are you doing here? You should be with the other *interns*," Influencer Anastasia rudely scoffs at Deslin and I.

"Isn't the Body Imaging Centre down there?" Deslin prods back with one of his charming grins.

"Nice one, pretty boy. I'm a top Influencer here. Don't even try those charming tricks with me," Influencer Anastasia stares him down and squints, as if she's trying to insinuate some kind of staring contest.

My hands rummage through the rough knots Deslin helped to make in my hair, while he clears his throat. We don't dare say bye to Influencer Anastasia, let alone to one another, and proceed to sink back into the mirror corridor.

I return to a light tan girl fiddling with a tablet and range of developing story boards on my desk.

"Girl, you better tell me everything that just happened to make your cheeks all rosy red like that!" Zasha says a little too loud.

I roll my eyes but feel secretly grateful that I have someone to talk to about this. I've been over the *gotta pretend to be fake and unattached* thing ever since Influencer Jeenz confided in me.

For some reason, Influencer Jeenz is in the Communications and Analytics Department. She motions for me to follow her.

"Just a sec, Zasha. I have to do something real quick," I hurriedly say.

"Oh my god. Why are you always disappearing? You really don't like me, huh?" she dramatically says, fluttering her sparkly lashes and flipping around her long, wispy locks in my face.

I sputter and chuckle from getting whipped by Zasha's hair. Getting attached to people does make things harder, but that's just the risk I have to take. I quickly jog to where Influencer Jeenz is, sinking into the mirror corridor together toward the Beauty Bio Space.

Flying past Deslin and the curly haired guy I remember as Jrelito, Influencer Jeenz yanks me into her office as soon as she sees me doing a double take. When I open my mouth, Influencer Jeenz puts a finger on it to stop any words from flowing out. Her intently staring eyes pierce right through me. I might be me projecting, but she seems to look a bit worried.

"Don't say a word. We can't speak here. It's not safe anymore," Influencer Jeenz aggressively whispers.

She grabs my hand and thankfully, the office is enclosed with mirrors from the outside so that nobody can see what's happening inside. I guess it's not as soundproof as Influencer

Jeenz would desire, though. She pulls open a hidden bottom drawer of her desk and takes out a few mirror tiles all resembling shapes and sizes of different body parts.

"What are y-" I start to say but am soon interrupted by a sharp glare from Influencer Jeenz.

She can surely be ferocious, but at least she's respectable. I just hate when she hisses at me as if I have no idea what I'm doing.

On the floor, Influencer Jeenz begins arranging the mirror tiles into a shape that somewhat reflects a human body.

She whispers something to herself, something about *the end.* The tiles start to itch toward one another and all float up slowly in the air, finally uniting together as one whole body. A gorgeous, beautiful body that seems to belong to.... *Influencer Jeenz?* All of a sudden, I hear a cracking sound and see chromatic shards rush to the ground.

"Hellooo? Why are you looking at the floor? Let's go!" Influencer Jeenz says, waving her hands in front of my face.

I look up only to see that a glowing, gaping mirror door had replaced the mirror tiles in the middle of the room. We walk in together, the world goes blank for a bit, and we find ourselves in a dome-shaped oval room.

"Welcome to where all the magic happens, where Speculo's history has been created, repeated, mourned, and forgotten about. Welcome to Ovatus," Influencer Jeenz sighs, with a certain distinction of nostalgia in her voice.

We both plop down on the floating saucer chairs. It's been a long day for the both of us it seems.

"I brought you down here because I realized that we need to start being much more secretive for the future. Now, thanks for gathering information and seeing the opinions of current Mirror Mania staff, but it's time to really get to work now."

She's always so straightforward and to the point. It's annoying, but I guess effective.

"No problem. I'm ready for anything. What do I need to do?" I eagerly ask.

Influencer Jeenz is staring me right in the face again, as if she's about to admit something extremely confidential.

"Well. This is our most important, most crucial assassination yet. It is called The Traction Project for security purposes."

A lump in my throat starts to form and my face feels hot. It's still weird to imagine myself as an *assassin*.

"Right! So, who is it then?" I ask, trying to maintain my eagerness.

Influencer Jeenz is still staring at me dead in my eyes, but her gaze is even stronger now. Sometimes, I really think she doesn't like me, but maybe that's just how she is.

"Influencer Anastasia," she says without a single twitch in her defined face or slender body.

She pauses to look at me but continues to speak.

"Now, Ovatus is a fairly new organization. It's been changed over the years from previous names, but what matters now is that assassination is a relatively new objective. There are others. I will introduce you when the time comes. You will be gaining more leadership and I need to know if you are willing to handle that."

My face flusters and I start tapping my finger against the smooth surface of the chrome seat. Of course, I'm damn ready! I've been ready! Shojan always tells me *forgiveness,* but what good is that when I can take out one of the most influential Influencers of Mirror Mania, constantly belittling everyone? What good is *forgiveness* when this stupid system made me feel like I wasn't worth forgiving *myself?*

"I'm in. Like 100 percent. How exactly do we plan to carry this out? Who else is involved? Why is Influencer Anastasia so powerful anyway? Can you tell me more about The Traction Project? How are we going to do this again?" I continue running my mouth.

Influencer Jeenz slowly nods her head in approval and gives an attempt at what I think is a supportive grin. Her affection lasts as short as a blink.

"It is apparent that you are quite excited. That is a solid sign. As I said, you will be receiving further instructions and more leadership soon. Deslin knows quite a bit, so you can speak with him as well. Ovatus and its predecessor names were created to essentially check Mirror Mania. As things have gotten out of control, Ovatus now wants to take a stance. Anastasia and I, well were actually, best friends. Well, Anastasia, Brecky, and I," Influencer Jeenz clarifies.

Eventually, the words just come out of my mouth before I can fully think about what I'm saying, but I decide to just surrender to the present.

"Alright, so because you guys aren't best friends anymore, you want to assassinate her?" I confusedly ask.

"Obviously incorrect. Well, Anastasia needs to be assassinated because she now holds most of the power, despite me being the head. She's the one who has the control. She's been secretly performing experiments on Speculo residents above their maximums and below their minimums. The reason why she's gotten so much power is because all the other Influencers are proponents of using everyone that is not at their midpoint as a source of humor," Influencer Jeenz elaborates.

"That makes more sense, I guess. That is disgusting and inhumane. I'm surprised Influencer Ubili wasn't the one caught doing that. One thing I still don't get is why you, the

Head of Mirror Mania, want to even change or destroy this place? You have it the best!" I let out.

"Well, let's just say that I am sick of this so-called paradise. The pressure to constantly be perfect is no longer appealing to me," Influencer Jeenz primly says, somewhat offended that I didn't fully understand her reasoning the first time and shouldn't continue prying.

Influencer Jeenz gracefully stands up, straightens out her ultra-tight, waist-clenching skinsuit, and clasps her hands together.

"Well then, Ropashna. Let our most drastic assassination begin."

I nod my head as professionally as I can and purse my lips.

"As a side note, I thought it might be beneficial for you to know that your desk mate Zasha is involved in The Traction Project as well," she adds, standing above me with no desire to display any sign of empathy.

Heat infiltrates my body again, and the room suddenly feels too stuffy. Ignoring my growing agitation, we both go back the way we came in. After leaving Influencer Jeenz office, I stare at myself in the mirror covering, realizing just how intense of a commitment I just made. I see a familiar figure appear behind me.

"Well, what was that about?" Zasha intrudes.

I stare at her long and hard, not knowing if I should get angry that she's been lying to me this entire time. Why am I mad? I don't have to hide from her anymore. Isn't this what I've always wanted? Maybe, it's because I wanted to be the only one. I wanted to find a reason to be alone, so that I could take the credit and not have to compete with anyone.

"Don't worry about it. Did you finish your feature article about the latest waist trainer that melts pounds off in just thirty-eight hours?" I ask out of an attempt to mask my annoyance.

I regret my question as soon as I ask it but take her tablet anyway because I can be a people pleaser at times.

"I did! It's great! We should both buy them. Maybe we can both buy them for each other!" Zasha squeals in delight.

I roll my eyes but can't help but casually smile. She can't tell I'm angry.

Distraught by the recent conversation between me and Influencer Jeenz, I decide to message Deslin on Facegram.

"Hey, juicy lips. I need to tell you something," I message.

"First off, that's racist. Second, what's on your mind?" He responds.

"I don't know if Influencer Jeenz has already talked to you, but it seems that our plan is starting a lot sooner than we thought," I say, deliberately trying not to include anything about assassinations or The Traction Project.

He reads it but doesn't respond for a few minutes. *Did I speak too much?* I think, while checking my tech button every twenty seconds.

"Yeah. I'm aware of some stuff. I didn't know you knew," he types.

I furrow my brows and start reading way too much into his message.

"What stuff do you know? And why would I not know? She told me you knew a lot!" I message.

"She and I have been working more together. That's all. I'm glad you're on board. We were both nervous you would pull back, so that's why I'm surprised she told you already."

I decide to *not* assume the worst. Why would they think that *I, of all people,* would pull back?

"Yup! I guess we're really doing this then! :)" I type back.

I shut my tech button off to bask in everything that just happened. A few minutes later, I check Facegram to see if there's a response from Deslin. I turn my tech button off again, and the cycle repeats for about an hour until I finally get a notification: *Deslin liked your message.*

I feel my insides bubbling and blazing even more with the realization that I'm already getting attached to someone that I don't even know that well. I realize that there's too much at stake to be worried about how much a stupid boy likes me.

CHAPTER 10

COMPLETED AGAIN: DESLIN

———

Sometimes, I feel like I'm a celebrity intern at Mirror Mania and I must admit that it feels damn *good*. The attention, the batting eyelashes, and even the dudes feel intimidated by me; *my dick feels gigantic*. I honestly didn't think that the Beauty Bio Space would be a place where I would thrive, but I mean, I do pretty much thrive anywhere. Especially with these rock-hard abs. Today is my day off from the internship, but I might consider going in anyway. Maybe, I'll run into Ropashna or Jeenz.

"Oi Deslooo! Breakfast is ready!" Aama calls.

My warm arms stretch out, as I jump out of my Tesmo and throw on a tattered orange kaftan. Bolo, my favorite rapper, starts firing up some verses from my tech button. I quickly smash my alarm off and check Facegram.

"Heeeyy sexyy," I message Ropashna.

"Hey! ahah."

Damn, that was fast. She's really into me, huh.

"It's been a while. Miss that ass. How you been? Miss me?" I say.

Cocky or confident?

"Yeah, I'm doing well. Just been working on the plan and all. Also, pro tip: Influencer Anastasia and Influencer Brecky are a lot smarter than they look."

"Look atchu. Hard work is sexy. And what do you mean? Are they getting suspicious?" I ask.

Huh, the other Influencers might be fighting back. I didn't even think they would have a clue about the assassinations, but I guess you can only say so many people have been *abducted* for so long.

"You think everything I do is sexy! But, yes. They're catching onto us. I heard something about expanding markets or something like that. We should probably talk about this in person," Ropashna texts back promptly.

An immense amount of heat rushes to my face, and I release my building rage through a knuckle-cracking punch at my Tesmo's electric blue gel outing, rippling and shaking my entire floor. The smell of freshly boiled poken fills my wide nostrils while I gallop down the stairwell, but I feel my mother's toned arms embrace me before I can fully appreciate the luxurious scent of her skills.

"My Desloo! Come eat, eat, na," she gestures me to our dining table without loosening her affectionate grip.

Today, the dining table is a mahogany wood table, decorated with silver plates and bright yellow and red napkins: the three colors of the Contra flag. One of the buttons on the side of the table allows Aama to change the layout of the table whenever she wants, but I guess she must be feeling homesick today.

"Desloo. I haven't talked to you in a while. How is your internship going?" Aama sweetly asks.

"I've been busy working, yeah. It's quite interesting, though. I've been learning a lot about the assasi—I mean real world," my mouth sputters.

My eyes blink hard and are afraid to open again in fear that Aama would see right through them. However, the clashing of her navy-blue cast-iron pans slightly ease my concerns. I like how Aama continues to cook in a very old-fashioned way sometimes, delicately grinding her own vibrant spices and using ancient, yet completely foolproof, techniques.

"Heay? I can't hear you, my Desloo! The air from the electric fan is too loud! It seems that you are happy, though. I am glad you are home because it's a special day today, you know that, right?" she vehemently screeches, somehow still sounding cheerful and affectionate at the same time.

That's why the table is all decorated, and why she's been slaving away in the kitchen more than usual.

"How could I forget? It's Papa's birthday!" I enthusiastically shout back to her from across the room.

Aama glances over at me to raise her eyebrows, letting me know she knows my enthusiasm is not legitimate, opening her mouth to scold me, but a tall and dark wrinkly figure prevent words from exiting her mouth. His natural frown slightly lessens, and his hazel pointed eyes scan the room, calculating the imperfections of the room.

"Hello," he booms, as if passive aggressively signaling Aama to hurry up and get food on the table in the next five seconds or a shit storm would ensue.

Already planted at the opposite side of the table, I look up from the floor and try to make conversation.

"Happy fiftieth birthday, Influencer Ubili."

"I'm surprised that you're even here right now. Don't you have work to do?" he questions, clasping his rough veiny hands, while adjusting his dull black and grey twined curls.

Knowing that I would take a bit to respond, his gaze darts toward Aama, notifying her to pick up the pace even more. Stumbling with trying to balance trays of delicately wrapped poken, fire glazed hazelnut shrimp, and handmade cassava rolls, Aama wipes her sheeny forehead and satisfyingly slinks into a seat near the middle of the table.

"You never cease to amaze me, Aama," I praise.

"We'll see. Today better be special," the opposite side of the table grunts.

Aama gently curls her thick lips, shyly moving her eyes around the room, patiently awaiting her judgment.

Papa gingerly presses the other table button: *swoosh!* A rush of air pops out in the gaping hole of the table for three hot and sparkling clean plates and cutlery instantly appear. Papa reaches for his plate and cutlery first. He always takes his plate first and serves himself.

Intentionally picking impoverish samplings from each dish, he returns to his seat. I get up to serve myself, but Aama widens her eyes, pleading for me to let her receive Papa's approval first and foremost. This shit happens every time, and they wonder why I'm barely home. This is why Ropashna doesn't even know much about them.

The rude clicks of Papa's long, creepy tongue surround the dining room, while he carefully stabs a piece of shrimp for it to barely dangle on the edge of his fork almost entranced, as if he is back in the Beauty Bio Space operating. He nods once at Aama, squints his eyes, slurping in her art. We all hear him swallow and gently let out a sigh, slowly opening his mouth for his thoughts to manifest out loud.

"Scrumptious, my love. You impress me. Sometimes."

Screeechhh. Aama shoves the chair away, almost scraping her ankle from dire excitement, and squeezes Papa's broad, bony shoulders. After smattering about seven juicy and prominent smooches all over his rumpled forehead and crinkly cheeks, Papa shoos her away by giving her his plate to fill it enough so that he won't be hungry for the rest of the afternoon.

"So, tell me, Deslin, what exactly do they have you doing at Mirror Mania? You have been working hard, no?" Papa asks.

I look straight into his hazel eyes as if I'm looking into a mirror of myself.

"You know I already am. I pretty much do the same thing you do," I let out.

Papa raises an eyebrow, while scratching his practically non-existent goatee. He clears his throat and forcefully slams down his fork on the table.

"The *same thing,* you say? Des, you ought to be an influencer yourself, you know. They're set for life! They're practically idols that society worships the perfection of the Mirror Mania lifestyle. Imagine that level of perfection! Your mother and I are getting old, you are our only child, and you being an intern already has you on this path, so I trust that you truly are working as hard as you can. I don't want you getting into any sort of trouble. No distractions," he lectures.

I nod my head, distracted by the steam and fragrance of all the delicious food in front of me. Aama finally sets Papa's plate down and hands me mine.

Dumping five freshly wrapped poken on my plate, I respond with directness, "Listen, you know I am responsible. You know I've always wanted this, alright? I will make you proud," I tell the growing warmth in my forehead that it needs to wait its turn to be released.

"Of course, Desloo! We just want to make sure. When you were younger, we all know they weren't the best of times. We just want to make sure your intentions at Mirror Mania are pure," Aama chimes into the conversation.

"Deslin, just don't waste our time and your time. I've been hearing all this talk about some kinds of assassinations or abductions. Some crazy nonsense about Mirror Mania where there shouldn't be a standard of how much we should all weigh and look like. There's even talk about people going against the standards and dietary rules Speculo has followed for so long, something called 'listening to their bodies.' It's truly insane! Why take so much effort to listen to ourselves when we could be wrong? Influencers are influencers for a reason. They have been guiding us for so long, and I just want you to be one of them because I know you are an exemplar leader," Papa says in a blunt, yet somehow appraising, way.

The oozing white liquid travels around the poken sitting in my plate. I really don't know what to say because that was probably the most sentimental thing, he's said all year to me, but also for the more obvious reason that I've been lying this entire time.

"Yes. I agree. I appreciate your concern, both of you. I know I'm capable, but I need the Head Influencers to see that, and I have to keep proving myself. It's just going to take some time," I reassure them.

It's not like I haven't lied to them before.

"Anyway, these abductions or so-called assassinations, or whatever the hell they are! At first, I thought it was just a ploy because the Beauty Bio Space needed more participants for research *activities*. Key Influencers have gone missing, however," Papa continues to ponder.

I continue tasting the creamy delicacies that Aama put her full heart into.

"Definitely. By the way, how come I don't really see you around Beauty Bio Space?" I ask instead.

Changing the topic to himself is a great way to deviate.

"I come in on my own time. I'm old, like I said. Most of the time, I'm just on call," Papa boringly says.

Right, Papa. That's why he still makes me call him Influencer Ubili most of the time.

Aama flashes an innocent smile and Papa purses his purplish lips in some twisted way to display his contentment. After we finish eating, some family and friends arrive for celebratory coffee and air cake in the living room. With an apparent lump in my throat and inability to distract myself from our conversation, I open my tech button screen.

"Traditional Contra playlist on surround sound. Low medium level," I whisper with conviction to my wrist.

Light drums and melodic hums rush into the room, eventually settling in peoples' twitching legs and black-haired head bopping. For a little bit, I forget about the pressure. For a little bit, I'm just a guy who's celebrating his Papa's birthday. For a little bit, there's no assassinating Influencer Anastasia. There's nothing but the music, the rhythm, the beat. And I'm just me.

Only for a little bit though, because Jrelito's name replaces the melodic lyrics. I take our conversation back to the kitchen; his penetrating emerald eyes pop out in front of me.

"Hey man. I wanted to see what you were up to. Can I come over?" Jrelito asks on the miniature screen projection.

"Honestly, fuck it. Come over. I'm just with family," I say.

"Ayyy, you better have some cute ass cousins!"

I shut off my screen before my rage speaks. Not about Jrelito, but about everything that has happened and has been happening. As I make my way back to the living room, Papa winks at me because the whole room is filled with cousins and aunties and uncles who are somehow drunk off coffee and are dancing to some old shit that Papa sung back when he was my age.

Making my way to the center of our light oak floor, I tap my feet to the beat. Black shiny-haired heads swish over and uncles start slurring their words. My arms strongly push and pull the air around me. Strong and *controlled*. My closest cousin joins me, moving our feet together in unison now. *Wooo!* The room cheers. I miss when it was this easy to be happy. To be seen as successful, talented, just because you danced in front of a roomful of family.

After my heart beats begin to overpower the thumping in my brain, I go sit on an uncomfortable wooden chair next to Aama. Observant, but with radiantly plump cheeks, she turns to me.

"I love your father, but sometimes I don't know if that's enough," she quietly says.

I look into her eyes and we both recognize the feeling of never being good enough. We both know that no matter if we're at our perfect midpoint weight, we have the most toned arms, flawless skin, anything, that we just would never be good enough for him, for Speculo, for Mirror Mania.

Taking a risky assessment of her vulnerability, I genuinely ask, "Aama, do you feel like all this pressure to be perfect, all this pressure to be an Influencer is really worth it?"

"Desloo, you know I am supposed to say 'yes' just to keep things civil with your father. I want you to be happy. That's all I've ever wanted, actually. I do think you being an

Influencer would make you happy, my Desloo. Your father and I... we didn't grow up with much. We lived every day worrying if we would even be able to eat dinner that night. I just... I really never want you to experience that," she says with glistening eyes.

Mothers. They lie to you, and then get away with it because it's all for you. Or so they say.

I simply nod my head in agreement, but our conversation is halted because Jrelito pops in through our open, silvery mesh door.

"Ayyy! What a party!" He immediately breaks out.

He charmingly greets Aama with a kiss on her petite hand and gives birthday wishes to Papa. With much hesitation and many overly forceful tugs on his icy blue striped skinsuit, I finally drag him outside for a walk.

"Brooo! I wanted to scope out one of yo fine ass cousins, especially that shawdie in the lil' tight red dress. Like oooh gawd dayum, that ass! Why we out here in this dank neighbor-hood, anyway?" Jrelito goes off like an instant flying tractor.

"Listen, I just don't wanna be in that house right now. There will be plenty of opportunities for you to meet my cousin, or cousins for that matter. I already wished my Papa for his birthday and all, but I wanted to talk to you about something really important," I say.

Somehow chewing on some random ass jalapeño-infused protein pork rinds, Jrelito takes a few moments to respond.

"Yeah, I'm here for you. What's up?" he abruptly rests to sit on a dusty chromebox perched on the sidewalk.

I sit on one next to him, wincing as the chromebox's cold dewiness splurges across my backside. I debate opening up to him about all the pressure, but I'll save that for Ropashna because this dude is probably just gonna think I'm just a pussy. I probably am, but that doesn't mean I have to hear it from a dude that chomps on fake animal fat bits to grow his non-existent biceps.

"We been friends for a while, and I guess I just wanted to know if you know anything about the abductions or supposed assassinations that are going on" I lead.

"Yeah! I thought you would know because you're pretty well-versed with everything that goes on and you're hella close to Influencer Jeenz. Why you asking?" he says.

"Well, yeah I am. I just wanted to ask your opinion on it and all," I say, nonchalantly shifting my chromebox's position to more reclined setting.

"I support it. Who wants to live like this? Eating fake shit all the time just to maintain some fake number? I've been actually gathering with some other dudes and chicks in the Beauty Bio Space."

Interesting. All this time I thought that whispering was all about how fine I looked in my tight black skinsuit.

"I guess Ovatus hasn't really been that much of a secret then, has it?" I test Jrelito further.

"Bro! We already know. We already know you're part of it, hell, even at the forefront. Influencer Jeenz literally ONLY talks to you out of the interns in public and basically growls when she sees the rest of us. We're not stupid, even if that's what you think," Jrelito says, his tone dripping with pure honesty.

He's part of Ovatus too? Damn, I would have thought Jeenz would have told me that.

"When did you even get started with Ovatus?" I incline to Jrelito.

Jrelito stops chewing and his vivid green pupils dilate out of both fear and excitement.

"Hold up! Check this out!" Jrelito dodges my question out of his lack of concentration skills.

His beefy fingers point to posts on Facegram of famous Influencers and well-known midpointers of Speculo affirming the assassination rumors.

"God damn, bro! Influencers and midpointers are real angry that the rest of Speculo fighting back, eh? The posts be saying that Mirror Mania is gonna increase security measures or some dumb shit. Damn, even Influencer Anastasia out here saying that the assassinators will be punished," Jrelito explains.

I don't even think there will be enough time for Influencer Anastasia *or* Mirror Mania to fully prepare for what's coming.

"Anyway, yeah. I got involved with Ovatus even before I became an intern. My parents chill and they all about peace and equality and all that, so we been trying to check Mirror Mania, even change it, for a while now," Jrelito continues.

"If you're all for peace and all that, then how are you just fine with assassinating Influencer Anastasia?" I ask.

Jrelito dives his hands into the remaining crumbs of his environment dissolvable, toxin-free bag of pork rinds.

"I mean there was definitely a lot of discussion 'bout dat one. We look at it this way. We been trying to be the good guys for so long, and it's not working. We gotta step up the game, make a real statement. Never thought that would be violence, but I think of it as justice, not destruction" Jrelito says in the most sophisticated way I've heard him speak yet.

In silence, we both look out into the deep violet tones of the night sky. Mirror Mania's building still shines and a few, freshly polished droids march in the distance.

"For sure. Good to know I'm not in this alone," I finally say.

"You never have been, man. You just Mr. Someone Better Remove This Stick Up My Ass," Jrelito pokes back.

With crinkled eyes and brotherly grins, we shake our heads and chuckle together. After we both run back home, I decide to call Ropashna for a bit before sleeping off the unexpected craziness of today.

A yawning, pixelated girl appears in front of my driveway.

"Ah, Deslin? Hi-hi... I was just about to sleep," Ropashna greets me.

"I just wanted to see your face," I say with a deep sigh, anxious if I'm saying the right words.

The growing frostiness of the air gracefully chills my bare arms. I keep feeling so anxious and awkward around her and I don't know why. It wasn't like this before.

"Ah, did you have a good time at your Papa's birthday?" Ropashna says, straightening herself up behind a wooden headboard.

"It was good. Jrelito came over actually," I say, trying to force myself to open up, but the wind seems to suffocate me instead.

Why is it so hard to tell her these things all of a sudden? I feel so bad for sounding like a dick who doesn't seem interested.

"You seem really tired. I am too, so I'll honestly just see you soon. Good night!" Ropashna blows a cute kiss on the screen.

This pressure of Aama and Papa, working with Jeenz, feeling like a hypocrite for actually liking the Beauty Bio Space sometimes, thinking Ropashna and I could be something, it's all just too much. Girls come and go, but this opportunity is what I've been waiting for my entire life. It was all so simple when I started this Internship program, and that's where I need to go back to.

CHAPTER 11

THE TRACTION PROJECT: ROPASHNA

Influencer Jeenz and I have been working together for a while, but I still feel like she holds herself back from me. I feel like there's more to her than just her perfectly sleek, velvety locks. She's too clean, too perfect; there's something missing.

"Oiii Ropaaa!" Mom calls from downstairs.

I immediately flop my tangled braid over my shoulders, flouncing down the spiral staircase and letting my fingers delicately glide over the coppery tones of mixed wood, being careful not to indulge my skin with splinters. Instead of seeing Mom's silvery bun and dusty grey apron at the door, Zasha's violet eyes and her traditional Sunare paisley-printed jacket peer at the front door.

"Haven't you invaded my privacy enough?" I half joke, but Mom doesn't understand and walks toward the kitchen as an excuse to raise her voice.

"ROPA! How dare you speak like that! Come down here," Mom says with exasperation and confusion as to how I could be so entirely hostile toward my supposed best friend at Mirror Mania.

"Ropashna... why are you so upset? I thought you would be *excited*, girl! C'mon, we can be assassins *together*. Isn't this what you always wanted? You don't have to hide from me anymore. You don't have to hold back!" Zasha's squealing voice echoes, along with the grumbling of her gerbil sized stomach.

"Hey! Don't be so loud! Mom and Dad just found out about this and they're still confused," I whisper, praying Mom's ears didn't decide to perk up at one of her random times. "Anyway, why didn't you just tell me earlier?" I continue to ask out of curiosity, rather than resentment.

"The same reason you didn't tell me! I didn't know if I could trust you...I also know I don't look like I struggle with loving myself, but I do," she easily admits with a shrug, careful not to dote on her self-depreciating efforts.

"Of course, you do," I say with a slight smile.

"C'mon, girl. I want us to work together. You're going to need the help," Zasha tries to convince me, winking in slow motion with one of her notoriously long eyelashes.

"You're right," I say, while pulling her in for a tight embrace.

Spying from the corner of the kitchen, Mom flashes a toothy grin and returns back on a delicious scented path of whatever new recipe she's decided to concoct for today.

"Anyway, how are *you* doing? I'm sure all of this pressure to take down an entire system is getting to you. A lot of the people in Ovatus know you, but you haven't even properly introduced yourself to them, you know," she says.

"I guess...it's like that feeling where 'this is too good to be true,' so you're just...numb. You don't really do too much because you're afraid that you'll lose the opportunity," I say, a bit confused on how everyone already knows me.

"But, if you do nothing, that's when you'll lose it, won't you?" She tilts her head to say, letting me know she's here for me.

"Affirming my fears," I say, nodding my head and sighing out of relieving the tension between us.

We're silent for a bit, but I want to keep letting out my feelings. She's always had such a way with opening me up, an effect I wish I could impose upon Deslin.

"Zasha, I feel like I am so bothered all of the time by random things, by the world and its current state, by my family's set ways of thinking. Sometimes, I just wake up *bothered*. I don't know what it is. Maybe it's part of who I am. Maybe I've *let* that become part of who I am," I start babbling.

"Gosh! It is just too much energy to be so bothered all the time, ya know. I think happiness is a choice sometimes. I know that I make it look easy, but I realize that it's not," Zasha says in a much more understanding tone.

It's nice to see that she's kind of like the rest of us...kind of like me, at least.

"It's not even just you, Zasha. It's this...entire...fucking place. We're taught that it's *easy* to be *healthy, to be happy,* to buy into this idea of perfection. It's like we're living back in this Greek and Roman age of humanism, but in such a less overt way," I keep on going.

I finally can let out all of the feelings and thoughts I've been having since Orientation, since the Masquerade, since Ovatus—everything.

"Interesting! I never really thought of it like that, but I suppose that is true. Why do you think that is?" Zasha ponders, rubbing at her barely-there peach fuzz on her chin.

"I think the world is just a culmination of our projected selves. The way we act toward ourselves, what we expect and think of ourselves is physically manifested in society through popular values, activities, food. Humans have been *obsessed* with this notion of perfection for centuries, yet we all know it is scientifically impossible to achieve," I surprise myself with how coherent and sophisticated I sound.

Maybe I've been spending too much time with Influencer Jeenz.

"People won't listen to you unless you have money because money is the physical embodiment, the most simple and overt form of evidence, of power," I babble, no longer feeling like I'm not just talking to Zasha, but to myself now.

"I agree for the majority of the time, but look at you, Ropa. You are not the perfect midpoint weight, yet you decided to fight anyway. You're in the process of leading an entire revolution. I think people actually listen to those that are unafraid and truly accept themselves for who they are, because that's true power. Influencers can influence, but individuals coming together can create lasting change," Zasha says, surprising me with how coherent and sophisticated *she* sounds this time.

"You should sound smart like this more. Maybe, you'd be the one leading this thing instead," I lightly joke.

The room sensationally rings with her laugh, a knock on the door, and a slight buzz from my tech button.

"Can you let me in?" A message from Deslin appears on my notification window.

I turn toward Zasha's heart-shaped and flawless, natural face. She already knows who it is.

"I want to talk to him sometimes, but I also know it won't go anywhere because it's not like I can talk to him about the things I actually want to talk about. I used to think that it was some hidden code that you couldn't, but it's more so we aren't on that intimate level anymore. That level of trust and comfort disintegrated or honestly, maybe it was really never even there to begin with. He always had some barrier up," I continue letting out to Zasha.

I didn't know it was this easy to just talk to someone like this. It's nice to share all this emotional burden.

"Wow. I didn't know you were so cheesy! That's literally the most senti thing you have said, girl," Zasha smirks, but says in a tone of gratefulness, as if she's been waiting for this kind of intimacy with me since Intern Orientation. "But, honestly. Just open the door. You want to talk to him, and you're not weak for that," her bright eyes gently blink at me with encouragement.

Twisting the door open, Deslin's sheeny dark skin, complemented with a bright blue muscle tank, haunts my view.

"I was just finishing up zooming around Speculo," he breaks the silence, waiting to be invited in.

"Hey, Deslin! What's up?" Zasha casually chimes in.

"I wanted to talk to you about plans in Ovatus and stuff Jeenz was telling me. Zasha, it's great that you're here too. The more of Ovatus around, the better," Deslin says with a certain type of coldness he portrays whenever talking about Mirror Mania.

"You sound like a robot, but sure," I reluctantly say.

"Welllll, I guess that's my cue to leave!" Zasha halfheartedly jokes and zips out the door with a wink and pat on Deslin's head, in which he returns with a disapproving grimace.

"Ropaaa! Did someone else just arrive?" Mom calls.

"Uh yeah, just a... just another friend," I hesitantly say.

"Hm. A friend. That's one way to put it," Deslin mumbles under his fresh, minty breath.

"You've never introduced me to your family. I bet you haven't even talked to them about me," I snap back, feeling obligated to introduce him to Mom and Dad.

"I mean, we aren't completely together, right? It doesn't really matter," he says in attempt to deescalate the situation or try to get away from being overly emotional in public.

"Do you really want to have this 'what are we' talk here?" I aggressively whisper back.

We shuffle upstairs without further continuing the conversation. Halfway through the stairs, he roughly tugs on my hand.

"Wait," he says with assurance, but somehow feels like he's looking out for me.

The lump in my throat softens.

"Hm?" I say, feeling a bit lighter in my voice.

"Um… maybe we should just talk on the way to Ovatus," he promptly says, while awkwardly looking around.

I can never tell with him. It used to be so easy—to translate his thoughts, to know what was on his mind, but it feels like the entry is blocked. I slide past him down the stairs, gazing into his beautiful hazel eyes, and gently kiss his chiseled, smooth cheek.

"Sure thing," I say.

A bit taken aback, he stumbles a bit down the stairs, proceeding to slip his off white zoomers back on.

Instead of taking a Bullet, we decide to zoom over to Mirror Mania instead, allowing the crisp Octeria air peacefully chill across my face. I remember Deslin telling me that Octeria is one of his favorite months because there's fewer people on the streets, making his zooms a lot more peaceful.

"Ropashna, don't you think Influencer Jeenz is so admirable? I think Jeenz is so smart," Deslin says before we enter Mirror Mania, saying Jeenz's name as if she's become a good friend, or maybe even something more.

He *has* been saying her name and not Influencer Jeenz for a while, now that I think about it. Another growing lump in my throat pays me a visit for round two. It's not my business; it's not like we're together.

"She is, for sure. I wish I knew more about her. It seems like her whole life is just Mirror Mania, and now Ovatus, I guess," I say, while we push inside the lobby entrance of Mirror Mania.

Deslin's rugged arms collide against my stomach from the momentum of the doors loudly shutting. His hazel eyes widen but soften just as swiftly. It feels nice to have a moment like this after what feels like such a long time, or maybe there's just so much to talk about that he feels so far away from me.

"Oh, sorry about that," he rotates his arm backward and yawns.

"Deslin, what's going on? Why have things been so different between us lately?" I decide to crack open the awkwardness between us.

Instead of a reassuring answer, his words are replaced with a few familiar giggles and whispers. Deslin and I knowingly glance at one another: it's the weekend, so who else could be here right now?

"God, could you even think about destroying Mirror Mania? We have everything! We *are* everything," The interjection of arrogance does not seem like Brecky, so it must be Anastasia.

Clicking of heels resonate through the lobby. Deslin and I quickly dash toward the check-in desk, curling right next to each other to stay hidden and to be close to each other.

"I don't know, Anastasia.... maybe it's time for a... um... change? I mean I love Mirror Mania and everyone here, but, um, all I think about is food and how to stay at my perfect midpoint weight. It's becoming, um, obsessive," I overhear, paying close attention to the added pressure of my zoomers that could potentially squeak on the streak-free floor at any moment.

"No! I've been hearing some talk amongst the interns that Jeenz is in on this. Maybe even a few other influencers in Mirror Mania...None of the interns should even know that Jeenz is the Head Leader of Mirror Mania, but I have a feeling that cocky Deslin and annoying Ropashna might," Anastasia loudly clucks with disdain and annoyance that she's been left out of what's been happening.

Deslin nudges me, rolls his eyes, and opens his mouth to imitate Influencer Anastasia. Before I say anything, he quickly covers my mouth because he already knows I can't help but laughing at his lame jokes.

"What are they planning to even do? We should, um, maybe talk? All of us?" Brecky nervously questions, more so to calm her hyper anxious-self down than for Anastasia to answer her questions.

"Brecky, just focus on your magazine for now. I *know* something is up. I don't know what it is, but something will be happening soon. I just wanted to know if you knew anything," Anastasia admits.

Hearing the same rapid clicking of heels, or rather stilettos that are at least four inches higher than the tallest pair that I own, I quickly back away from Deslin and swiftly turn my head. I have to stop letting him play with me like this.

"Oh, it's you. Ropashna. *And* Deslin! Interesting to see you both here on a *weekend*," Influencer Anastasia's icy, blue diamond patterned contact eyes directly pierce through mine.

My mouth is paralyzed because all I can think about is Influencer Anastasia and if she overhead Deslin and I speaking.

"I mean, I am pretty well known in the Communications and Analytics Department. I'm the assistant editor for the magazine, so there are plenty of reasons for me to be here and check in with the editor in chief, don't you think?" I retort, looking around for Influencer Brecky.

"Oh! I wouldn't be so snark if I were you. Also, Deslin, you're looking sooo toned now! Influencer Ubili must be why you're so conscious huh," Anastasia smirks, while raising a nonexistent, patchy blonde eyebrow.

Before I manage to say anything back, Influencer Anastasia nods and leaves, swaying her tiny hips back toward the Body Imaging Centre.

"Wait 'til she sees what's coming," I let out to Deslin, finally being able to breathe normally.

"It's doubtful her eyes work if she's dead," he jokes, but with a dead and flat voice.

Deslin and I don't speak much on our way to Ovatus. We do the regular procedure to get there and arrive with the greeting of Jeenz's slightly tanned, but apparently toned, back. She spins around at the sound of Deslin's deep sighing, as if she's all too familiar with such a sound.

"Thanks for coming, guys. We have a lot to discuss," Jeenz announces with covertness, looking around Ovatus with alertness.

"Ropashna, I am going to request that you stop telling people about Ovatus. Brecky and Anastasia have told the rest of Mirror Mania about us, and the board wants to throw me off. They're gathering at this instant, discussing whether or not to banish me from Speculo City," Influencer Jeenz grimly says.

Somehow everything she says just never sounds that emotional, even if it's something that's so drastic, like this. I've never really been close to Influencer Jeenz, but that doesn't mean I want her *banished*.

"How do they know you've been in charge of the assassinations?" I ask.

"Have you not learned anything during this internship other than all of the chemical treatments we provide to enlarge your ass to be as gigantic as the moon?" Jeenz tilts her head with a passive aggressive smile to match her equally brash tone.

I have to stop myself from laughing because of how lame she sounds when she tries to be sarcastic. Deslin's hands twitch, but he stares at me to make sure I control myself.

"The media controls *everything,* which means Mirror Mania controls *everything,*" she goes on.

"No I know...I mean I've told my parents already. I've told friends. People want to join. People have been protesting. People have been writing letters. We can't just go dark now!" My voice attempts to squeeze itself past the tightness of throat, producing a strained and whiny sound that causes Deslin to wince.

I'm just so confused. Jeenz is the one who thought I was going to back out, yet here she is.

"Ropashna, I get it. Jeenz has a point. We want this to work, so we have to be patient. Only processed emotion, not organic emotion, will work when it comes to the Influencers," Deslin adds in a calculated voice.

"The only time they'll choose something processed, huh," I mumble under my breath.

Jeenz shoots me a sharp look and shakes her head, as if I'm not taking the situation seriously enough.

"So, what do we do now? What do we tell Ovatus and everyone involved in The Traction Project?" I ask, trying to actively listen now.

"You mean, what do *you* tell Ovatus?" Jeenz turns to me.

"Huh?" I ask with sincere confusion twisted in my reaction.

Suddenly a band of all kinds of people come marching out behind Influencer Jeenz. There are the tall, skinny interns that I remember from Intern Orientation, old and retired Influencers that still look like they belong in a Mirror Magazine photoshoot, Zasha, Deslin's curly redhead friend Jrelito from Orientation, and.... Shojan? What's *he* doing here?

What the hell is going on? First, Jeenz says she has to go hide because the rest of Mirror Mania is catching on, or at least that's what I think. Deslin is acting so weird, and Shojan is part of The Traction Project?

"What? There's a meeting today?" I ask, furrowing my brows, but immediately relaxing by accepting that today is just going to be full of surprises.

"For someone so motivated and determined to be part of all of this, you sure don't keep track of the necessary details," Deslin sarcastically remarks.

I roll my eyes.

Influencer Jeenz's eyes widen as she hears more people falling in through the doors, realizing its her cue to slink back to wherever she was hiding before.

"I sincerely apologize about this rashness. Ropashna, I know you are ready for this. The Traction Project must succeed, regardless of Mirror Mania's reactions," Influencer Jeenz hastily whispers.

She briefly waves goodbye and disappears.

"She is so mysterious. Maybe that's why she is where she's at today. She probably doesn't let anyone get too close to her. She's the only one who knows the secretive parts about herself," I tell Deslin my observations.

"Maybe. I find it inspiring, honestly," he says.

His eyes appear misty adorned with an unusual, puppy dog look.

"Deslin, what is with you? You've barely touched me or spoken to me and you keep talking about how you're in awe with Influencer Jeenz," I look at him incredulously.

He lazily picks up my fingers, drooping our hands together for what I think is some kind of weird reassurance. Realizing that I'm now in control of an entire undercover project, a whole assassination scheme, the anxiety rushes over my body, and all I feel like doing is sleeping.

"Listen, I just think she's a great person. There are a lot of great people in this world that I don't want to be in a situationship with," he looks into my eyes and smirks his perfectly aligned teeth.

For some reason, the words are not special, but when he says them, they feel like it. More people enter, even families and young kids until the whole room is full. Deslin helps me mount myself on the floating platform. Zasha's wispy hair and Jrelito's shaking leg grabs my attention from the top.

"Helloooo, Ovatus!" I shout, trying to sound confident and assertive, but not arrogant.

I still feel sleepy and I feel my body swaying.

Chatter continues. Tablets and floating sticks with messy black ink sign the air with empowering phrases: *We are more than our body weight! Intuition over Influencer! We know our bodies!*

Instead of shouting for their attention, I let everyone bask in their common emotions for a common cause. I admire the beauty of it all: being part of something bigger than yourself.

It's a natural human desire. Everyone wants to contribute, but more importantly, everyone wants to feel like they've *actually* contributed.

"Ovatus. Thank you for showing your support. Thank you for bringing your posters, your comments, your loved ones. Thank you for everything. We have made tremendous progress!" I shout, letting my confidence shower the already glistening and gorgeous bodies of the crowd.

Everyone roars. Zasha smiles brightly and sticks up a thumbs up as high as she possibly can.

"I know you all must be wondering where Influencer Jeenz is. Sadly, she has gone into hiding because Mirror Mania has become extremely suspicious of her and the previous assassinations. From now on, I will be leading The Traction Project and Ovatus!" I say in a cheerful tone, immediately closing my eyes to pray that nobody will chuck their tablets at me.

There's some initial chatter, but then a few cheers from the crowd turn into rows of encouraging applause. Peeking open my eyes, I notice Deslin nodding his head that's glistening with sweat, urging me to say something that Influencer Jeenz would say. He's always loved just getting all the hard, emotional things done and over with, but that's where I shine.

"I need you all to listen to me. Mirror Mania is *listening*. They know about us. You are all part of The Traction Project for a reason. Influencer Anastasia's assassination will be the spark for lasting change in Speculo City! We all learned to trust ourselves and our bodies again, right? It's time for the whole city to do that!" I shout as loud as I have ever have before in my life with flaring nostrils and flushed cheeks to back me up.

I fixate on the eagerness and jumping within the crowd. The exciting energy of Ovatus fuels me.

"We've been planning this assassination for a while now. It's simple. The day that the Mirror Mania Magazine Issue is launched to the Speculo public, Influencer Anastasia is going down. We will be meeting shortly after today to discuss a detailed plan on what exactly needs to be done."

The room sings with screams and shouts of approval, further sparkling the room with pride and power.

Deslin glares at me, purses his lips, and glues his eyes to the floor. I don't have time or desire to deal with whatever his moodiness is about right now, so I leave him with a soft hug and shake hands with the other members of Ovatus. After everyone shuffles out, cheering and gathering around their friends and family, a familiar sandy brown head of hair waits for me.

"How come you never said anything?" I ask a little too enthusiastically, still hyped from the rallying energy of Ovatus.

"How come *you* never said anything, miss leader?" Shojan cracks back at me.

We smile and embrace each other tightly. He has a good point. I really don't want to make the same mistake I made with Zasha. What matters is that we're on the same side.

"I can't believe this is really happening, eh?" he says, wrapping a lanky arm around me.

"I can. We've finally found the perfect time to strike and there's no going back now," I say, affirming both belief in myself and Ovatus.

CHAPTER 12

KING JUNIOR: DESLIN

———

Who knew so many people were involved in Ovatus? Jeenz has decided that she wanted me to be her *personal assistant*, and I'm pretty excited. She's hot as fuck, she's got such a sexy body, and she's the leader of the rebellion. We've been working a lot more together and our flirty exchanges make me feel guilty sometimes, but Ropashna wouldn't understand if I told her. It's not her business, regardless.

"Brooo! How's it been?" I feel Jrelito's veiny, yet weirdly small, hands slap across my back that's still sore from yesterday's workout.

"Pretty decent. Just been working," I say, finger-combing through my sleek hair.

I glance up from my lab station and a few of the girls on the opposite side of the Beauty bio space look all flustered and flushed. I smirk to myself.

One new message from Ropashna!

"Heyy been a minute. What u up to?"

Her name makes me feel nervous, but not in the way it used to. I feel obligated, almost pressured.

"Working," I respond, trying to sound dry and uninterested.

I have to focus. She's a distraction. I can't let my family down.

"Ah I hope you aren't too stressed, you got this!" She responds back without hesitation.

Jrelito waves a camscope in my face, telling me to look at how to design bikini tops that use sweat to contour the body.

"Bro, who the hell uses these things?" Jrelito inquires, carefully examining the camscope's grotesque edges and numerous miniature buttons.

"The people that want to change themselves, or at least the ones that Mirror Mania believe need to be changed," I breathe, concentrating on extracting sample sweat particles on a spandex blend.

Zapping out of my focus, I realize how ambivalent I sound now.

"Deep Deslin, eh? That's what everyone is gonna call you in Ovatus now!" Jrelito lightly jumps around in a Contra footstep dance pattern.

"Speaking of, what's your thoughts on it all?" I rub my eyes and face him.

"Oh like the assassinations?" Jrelito innocently ponders, seeming to avoid further elaboration.

"You know you don't have to be so secret about being in Ovatus and just assassinations in general anymore, right? Everyone pretty much knows now. That's kind of the point for this whole thing to be successful, anyway," I blatantly say, somewhat attempting to make him feel more at ease.

I wonder why he thinks I'm so intimidating. I kind of enjoy it, though. His green eyes widen and he takes a second to think of an answer or a lie, maybe.

"Bruh it's crazy, but it is what it is! I mean, I'm not really too involved. That's for you and Ropashna to deal with, bro. As for Influencer Anastasia? Eh! I believe in y'all to take this shit down! I'm just here for moral support," Jrelito enthusiastically exclaims.

Right. I just don't know if it's Ropashna that I'll be doing this with anymore.

Just when I'm about to refocus, I feel a pointy tap on my shoulder from a set of perfectly white and almond-shaped nails.

"Heeyy! I thought I would come surprise you! I've just been running around to finish up distributing the magazines," Ropashna says.

Tilting my head back to establish some distance, my hand accidentally hits the conform chair's automatic positioning button to a more relaxed posture. I take Ropashna in. Curvy hips in a tight, white dress, somewhat chiseled triceps, and glowing brown skin with sweat on her leftover eyebrow hairs that resemble miniature ivory fat zap tool instruments.

"Stunning," I mumble.

"What?" she says with her big doe eyes twinkling with pure curiosity.

"Oh! I said where have you been running?" I flip my hair and hastily clear my throat.

"Running?" she catches on, putting her hands on her hips

She always does that when she seems to catch on to something. I find it simultaneously womanly and childish at the same time.

"Yeah. Running with your magazines. You should have at least let me catch a glimpse of you prancing around, clutching all those glossy covers to your chest," I flirt, trying to ease up the obvious tension between us.

Even Jrelito notices that distance between Ropashna and I lurks in the air, pushing him to the other side of the Beauty Bio Space, examining sweat glands of sacrifices and volunteers with the perfect midpoint weight. It's funny how in the end, we're all the same, but we just refuse to admit that.

"Alright, if I forgive you, it doesn't mean you have a probation period," Ropashna says, lifting one of her bushy, yet shapely eyebrows.

"Oh, I figured. For real, how's the distribution going? Any retaliation?" I ask with some interest, careful not to spend too much on the topic of repairing whatever we have going on between us.

"It's been going decently well. The rest of the town has received a lot of copies and I went to Influencers Brecky and Anastasia too. They looked at me like I was crazy, but Brecky seemed eager to read it. I feel like we can actually turn her on our side. Anastasia threw a massive fit and thinks that everything is fucked, so that's somewhat good. She said she was gonna make a loud ass announcement and throw out the interns who are involved with the assassinations and working with Influencer Jeenz," she elaborates as if she's been deprived of the chance to chat away in days.

I haven't really spoken to Anastasia, but she honestly doesn't seem that bad. She seems to be like she's not even fighting against our retaliation.

"Why don't you just call her Jeenz? You don't have to call everyone by Influencer," I say with agitation, partly out of hearing her voice continue to blab for so long and my interest in talking about something else.

It's like all we ever talk about and have been talking about is fucking Ovatus, as if we have nothing else to talk about anymore.

"Um, it's polite. What's it to you? Why have you been acting so off? Like what did I even do?" Ropashna instantly refutes back, with her rising tone alerting Jrelito's wandering eyes.

I really hope her fussing doesn't make me look stupid, especially not in the Beauty Bio Space.

"Listen. If you're going to be like this, then just go," I shoot back at her, monotone and straightforward.

Her eyes widen in rage, but then slowly droop in a way that I've never seen them before.

"Yeah, I'm gonna go soon. I just wanted to say that I have an official plan to assassinate Influencer Anastasia and I will be presenting to Ovatus tomorrow," she says with a virtually nonexistent voice inflection.

Before I can answer, Jrelito creeps up on us either out of procrastination or because he sees his boy out here needs some saving.

"Jeezzz! That's crazy, Ropashna! We makin' progress!" Jrelito pokes his head into the conversation.

Beeping sounds vibrate from Ropashna's tiny bulging wrist.

"Oh, looks like I have to go do some Ovatus stuff with Zasha. I'll see you guys later!" Ropashna winks at Jrelito.

Somehow, it doesn't really bother me.

"Don't ask," I turn to Jrelito, pursing my lips, and sliding around the sweat samples on my lab station, pretending to organize myself.

It's relaxing doing these experiments. It's as if only the science matters when I'm here. There's none of this picking sides, girls, parents, assassinating—there's no pressure. I actually think I enjoy being in the Beauty Bio Space.

"Wasn't going to. You know what's real crazy, though? Why isn't anyone going after Influencer Jeenz? Like, she's literally the leader of this whole shebang, yet you don't see Anastasia or the other influencers in MM who aren't involved going all batshit on Jeenz. Why is she so protected?" Jrelito asks.

"Dude, she's the leader of MM. Yeah, she's getting accused of the assassinations, but who would actually be able to take her down? People wouldn't even suspect that she has anything to do with this because of how much she preaches about Mirror Mania and the lifestyle it promotes. She doesn't even have a reason to assassinate or lead Ovatus, if you think about it," I say.

Hmm, she actually doesn't, now that *I* think about it.

"I have nothing to do with what?" a husky, but sexy voice emulates behind me.

Jrelito and I exchange delirious looks, wondering how Jeenz randomly could pop up out of nowhere like this.

"Oh, uhhh nothing to do with... crushing on Deslin! Aha!" Jrelito blurts in attempt to lighten the mood.

I shake my head, making our classic "bro, what?" face at him.

"You know... Jeenz, you know! All the chicks be *drooling* over this man, especially Ropaasshhnnaaa," Jrelito keeps ruthlessly digging.

"Hm. Not surprising," Jeenz calmly says with a slight smile.

"Yeah, I'm sure," I say with a chuckle.

"Regardless, I came to deliver this to you, Deslin," her hands glaze my desk with a sandy beige envelope. "Open it," she directs.

Tearing open the seal, a light grey letter plops out. These colors are already making me want to go back to injecting and examining real quick.

"Congratulations, Deslin. We would like to celebrate your promotion to *Head Assistant of Mirror Mania* with a secret dinner tonight at seven in the evening at Swirl Pub. We all look forward to congratulating you and enjoying delicious, macro-friendly pieces of food together. Best, The Influencers,"

I read aloud with articulation, feeling Jeenz intently watching my mouth.

I finish and see her shiny, pin-straight hair towering over me.

"I mean... thank you, but I have a question. I'm literally an intern, Jeenz. Why me?" I genuinely ponder with crinkled eyebrows.

"Why not you? Time does not mean so much. You're at your perfect midpoint weight, you have been loyal to your department and me, and you're probably one of the most attractive male members of Mirror Mania we have had in a while," she promptly says, yet spending a bit more time saying her last thought.

I bet those losers who called me a fat lard also really wanna suck my dick right now.

"Yeah. For sure. See you tonight," I nod, swiveling back in the conform chair.

"Looks really are everything in Mirror Mania, huh? Pretty boy out here getting all the power!" Jrelito colorfully comments.

"I mean, they do help," I play along.

Jrelito and I continue working on developing product samples for the public. We finish designing fresh and organic ingredient hand creams, injecting stored animal fat back into cheese, and adding back sugar and balancing macros to different snacks.

"Breaking the rules is *fun*," Jrelito emphasizes after a while, while struggling to extract whey from an old protein gummy worm.

I lose track of time until I check my tech button for any messages from Ropashna. Nothing. It's honestly good that I haven't received anything because I would probably be dry.

I want Ropashna, but it's just so much effort to maintain everything right now. She's this strong girl and I know she deserves my full effort, but I just don't think I can give that to her right now. Jeenz, at least, is simple. We spend time, we flirt, we work on Ovatus. I'll be working more with her now if this assistant promotion thing is actually true. There aren't so many feelings involved, but just enough to make me feel like I'm not alone.

"Good luck tonight, man!" Jrelito jumps out of his conform chair and gallops out all within a minute.

So much energy. All the time. So carefree. All the damn time.

After finishing up the remaining samples, I call for a Bullet and scan my arm across the shiny, black exterior.

Flying through the door to maintain my perfect first impression record, I frantically look for my maroon tuxedo.

"Eh! Desloo! You're home? I didn't hear you come in," Aama peeps her slightly wrinkly head into my room.

Feeling my annoyance and frustration from possibly being late, I pinch my hand to avoid yelling at her.

"Yeah, just getting ready," I grumble, throwing crumpled dress shirts and ties in all four corners of the room.

"What are you doing? Why are you in such a rush? Where are you going? Oh! Did you get a promotion? Do you want me to iron your clothes?" Aama clamors, standing right in the middle of my room now.

When I was younger, I would have snapped, but I know she's just excited. I'm grateful that I have a mother who cares so much.

Nodding my head as a response, while applying my remaining curl gel, I quickly call for another Bullet. Bustling back downstairs, Papa prevents me from my plans to make it perfectly on time.

Arms crossed, he asks, "Where are you going? Are you finally going on a date?"

"Why do you sound like Aama?" I roll my eyes.

"Why do you sound like a girl?" Dad retorts with a devilish sneer.

"I really gotta go." I push past him, stuffing myself outside before Aama can yell at me for turning my room into a tornado and Papa questioning me if I'm dating anyone.

A huge, swirly-shaped silver building entertains my view from the speedy bullet drive. Entering Swirl Pub, I immediately look at myself in one of the swervy mirrors. The mirror's ragged edges and a few broken shards distort my image into a short, chubbier version of myself. Does this reflect the current me or the old me? Floating tablets, droids, and silver tables encapsulate the room around me.

"Eerrrpp. Mr. Deslin. You Are Late." A bright silver mirror droid appears in front of me.

I criticize a small blackhead on my nose in one of its creepy, reflective eyes.

Taken aback, I say, "Uh, how do you even know me?"

"Go To Level Three Swirl Master Room," it conveniently ignores my question.

The thumping of my feet shakes the chromatic moving circles, causing mirror droid dude to shoot a reflection beam at me.

"Okay, I get it. I have a goddamn black head on my nose. I'll stop thumping," I murmur.

The droid immediately skates away leaving a fading streak on the floor.

Finally reaching the third floor, the room feels hard, decorated with multiple chandeliers dangling with chromatic shards and a large chromatic block in the middle with a touchpad circle of all worldly cuisines imaginable.

I suck in my cheeks to create my lady-winning smolder face and look to the left only to see Jeenz and her hair tied up into a tight bun with a few white stray hairs sticking out. Behind her, Influencer Anastasia, Influencer Brecky, and a few other influencers from Mirror Mania march to the chromatic block and level themselves on floating saucers. I wonder how Papa wouldn't know about all this, especially being so prominent in the Beauty Bio Space.

"I knew you'd be late, but let's get started," Jeenz motions to me that it's acceptable for me to join them at the circular dining table.

"We are all here today to celebrate Deslin and his new promotion to be my assistant!" Jeenz announces at a medium level.

Unamused, Brecky and Anastasia slowly clap. The rest of the Influencers don't bother to look up from their undistracted gazes at which cuisine they want to pick, calculating every single ingredient and measuring whether it'll be *worth* it.

"Oh, uh, thanks. Really. I've only been interning here for a bit, but it's an honor, Influencer Jeenz," I say with a bit of hesitation.

Swishing around her blonde beach waves, Anastasia speaks up.

"What exactly do you even plan to do with this... *boy?* Why him? We barely even know him!" she prods.

"Anastasia, did you order your food yet?" Jeenz politely responds with an underlying tone of aggression.

Surprisingly, Anastasia swallows her pride, despite probably not have eaten anything else since she found out I'm being promoted. She's so rude, but something about her attitude seems fake, or staged, almost. It's hard to assassinate her the more I interact with her, realizing maybe she's not so evil after all. The other influencers seem occupied with themselves;

some pull out their hand mirrors to double check their lipstick hasn't rubbed off yet and some take hand rulers to compare how sharp their jawlines are.

"I haven't eaten all day. I am absolutely *starving*," one of the random influencers says next to me.

"Girl, I hope they have all low carb stuff. I'm counting carbs again... the scale said I gained 0.5 pounds this morning. I'm not at my midpoint weight anymore. I gotta be real strict now!" another influencer adds.

I start to think about myself. Should I really be indulging myself? Will all the extra grease make me feel bloated and then I won't be at my perfect midpoint anymore? Will Jeenz regret her decision to promote me? Do I even deserve to be the goddamn assistant of Mirror Mania? It feels like I'm going against everything I thought I wanted to do when I first came here.

I shake my head to myself, confused with these insecurities that were only permitted to arise in a crowd that belittles me, not one that actually accepts me.

"Anyway... everyone! You can all stop staring or counting or examining or analyzing or whatever time wasting, scale pleasing thoughts you're having because I have actually done the honors of ordering everyone food for the rest of the night."

The table is silent, yet everyone's faces are frantic and full of fear. It's interesting when the power of choice is taken away from you, yet you would have made that same choice yourself.

"Um! Guess, um, it's.... cheat day!" Brecky screams as if it's her favorite celebration to exist.

In a spur, the voiceless influencers start congratulating me, pouring out their relief of choosing the most perfect option to maintain their midpoint weights. Anastasia even sends a warm smile across the table to me. Jeenz winks. My cheeks feel warm.

Just a moment later, droids march in a uniform line, bringing out an array of double-fried potato chips, strawberry-frosted white chocolate chip pancakes, deep-fried pizza sticks encrusted with crushed pork rinds, triple cream tomatoey pasta dishes—they're the most whole foods I have ever seen. No added protein. No sucked out fat. It's *all* there, just real gut-wrenching junk.

"I am *so* going to regret this," the same influencer next to me says, while stuffing a colossal heap of deep-fried pizza into her mouth. Her eyes flutter in harmony with the relaxed slump of her body, as if she's reached the most blissful state humanly possible.

I don't remember the last time I touched all of this shit. Possibly, when I was younger and sitting outside the gates of wherever my parents were. Jeenz glances at me, my full plate, and crumb-less mouth. Is she testing me? Is she trying to see if I can control myself? I watch her. She slowly drinks water, cleansing her palette by watching her workers as entertainment.

We have everything. We're idols who can eat anything, and that's the power everyone wants to have in Speculo. No wonder why Jeenz picked me, but why even go against Mirror Mania with Ovatus? Why would she want to take away this power? Everyone seems to obey her just fine. I push my plate away, stand up and make my way around the table looking at every single influencer in the eyes.

"You all are.... such a disgrace. Look at you! Gorging like pigs. You all are part of *Mirror Mania*. The place that preaches perfection and pure health. You hypocrites! You don't even deserve to be influencers. How could you betray the morals of

Mirror Mania like this?" I breathlessly let out from extreme frustration over my own conflicted feelings.

Chewing sounds disintegrate. Brecky's eyes fill themselves with water.

"I know! I know! It's, um, bad. I binge sometimes... I binge, um, once a week at least. I, um, just... I can't help it, okay?!" Brecky anxiously admits, as if she had admitted to being part of Ovatus to Anastasia.

I wouldn't be surprised, considering how everyone uses Brecky as a scapegoat all the time.

"Who else here binges regularly?" I ask around the table.

All the influencers hands raise, except Jeenz's. We lock eyes and smirk at one another.

"Well then! Do you all see why I made Deslin my assistant? We need to do better! We need to work harder! We are role models of Speculo. We embody perfection," Jeenz endlessly preaches.

I feel so much control. I feel so much power. With guilt and shame, the other influencers begin to nod their heads in agreement. Some of them furrow their brows, mentally berating themselves for failing to effectively refrain from gorging.

After a few more toasts of zero-calorie tea-infused sparkling champagne, a few others start dozing off, but Jeenz quickly finds a remedy.

"Well. How does it feel?" she immediately says to me loud enough for one of the sleepers to lightly flicker their eyes open.

"How did what feel?" I play along.

Jeenz points to the room, the droids, the floating saucers, the swirly mirror floor.

"Well, I see myself everywhere, so that's always a plus. It helps to have something appealing to look at, while testing my will power and food," I say.

"The greatest test of your life, I'm sure," Jeenz promptly responds.

"Jeenzzz, you know what I mean," I say, laying my head back from a practically empty stomach.

My eyes roll in annoyance, but I'm enjoying myself. I like the banter. She takes my mind of things.

"I don't know what you're experiencing. I only know what you tell me," she pokes.

Shrugging my shoulders at her words, I look into her deep emerald green eyes, and wonder why she even decided to become the head of Mirror Mania.

"Ah. Wonderful. Well, I will be blunt. I am sure you have caught on by now," Jeenz begins.

"That assassination stuff. Ovatus. It's all bullshit!" Anastasia comes into our conversation.

What the fuck? I had an itch that there was something strange, but I just didn't realize it would all be a ploy.

"What are you guys saying?" I decide to clarify, instead of aggressively accusing them.

"In short, we knew your class of interns was going to be problematic. Mirror Mania has always been gaining lots of *traction* with hate crime as well. So, we realized we must take it into our own hands. The already *assassinated* influencers, Anastasia, and I have been all discreetly working together," Jeenz crisply simplifies.

Involuntarily, my throat clenches and I don't know what to say. Why are they telling me this? Why even pretend to care? Who am I in all of this?

"Listen, Deslin. Everyone wants to feel in control. They want to feel like they have some kind of power, as if they have influence over what is happening," Jeenz continues.

"We're in *power*, so we get to decide what's happening! We're influencers! Speculo needs to be purified of these extremely below lowpoint and above highpoint freaks. That's what our secret little influencer group has been working on," Anastasia adds on.

I'm speechless, but also in awe. I didn't think the Influencers would be able to pull something off like this. It's all starting to make sense now.

"Jeenz, can I ask you something?" I turn toward her.

"Doesn't matter. You'll ask anyway," she jokes without smiling.

"Why? Why lead Ovatus and The Traction Project? Why appoint Ropasha?" I ask.

"Did you really think... I would give all of this up? Did you really think that I, of all people, the *leader* of Mirror Mania, would rebel on a system that privileges me the most? It's all for control. The Traction Project is simply a distraction, a pointless goal, so that us Influencers can maintain our power and continue eliminating worthless members from society," Influencer Jeenz cackles with excitement.

"Deslin, I have everything that I want. I love this life. I love the power. I made you my assistant because I saw myself in you, too. You just needed someone to see it in you." she comes closer, swaying her saucer closer to me.

I try to resist her charms, but she already knows my willpower is limited. Jeenz has been making moves on me for a while now, and it's already too late to go back. This is good for my image, this is good for my parents, and this is good for experiments.

"You of all people should be grateful. I know your family wants you to follow the Mirror Mania system, and I know how badly you want to make them proud. That little taste of power I let you savor tonight? That is how you will feel every day when you're working with me. Once again, Ovatus is a distraction for the little rebels, the ones that think they can change a whole corporation, a whole institution, a *whole way of living*," she whispers in my ears, sending shivers across my entire body.

Her luscious rosy lips stamp my shoulders, while her rose-colored manicured nails stroke my hair.

"Join me," she lustfully repeats, kissing my neck now.

Anastasia, Brecky, and the other influencers nod their heads in support, waiting for my compliance.

Simultaneously, I want time to both slow down, maybe even dip into the past, but I also want it to speed up. It's like we want the prosperities—not the experiences it takes to get them—but the reason we want them is because they are just a positive reminder of said experiences. I'm at the top now, and those stupid losers that bullied me as a kid can't do shit now. Papa can't even do anything if I join Jeenz and the Influencers side. Jrelito and Ropashna are temporary, but this is something I know I have to do.

"I'm in," I forwardly affirm, intently staring at everyone around the room.

I jump off my saucer, adjust my tuxedo, and charmingly nod at Jeenz. She stands there looking at me, as if she knows that I'll be back.

The glowing red letters of Swirl Pub twitch as I feel the cool breeze hit my face on the way out. It's dark out, it's late, but I try anyway.

"Can I see you right now?" I message Ropashna.

"What? Right now? I guess. Where?" she says.

"I don't care. I just need you right now," I sigh, impatient for a source of soothing distraction.

I shouldn't even be talking to her, but I know everything is going to change after today. There won't even be an us. There really isn't an us anymore anyway.

After a whole five minutes, she finally responds, "You're at MM still right? I'll just meet you outside."

"I'm actually at Swirl Pub," I say.

"What the...why?" she asks.

"Listen, just come," I half demand and half plead.

Ropashna liked your message.

While waiting for her, I wonder why Brecky didn't say much tonight. Is she even involved? Ropashna's flowing hair eventually emerges, following her curvaceous body wrapped in a sheer green top, white ripped jeans, and mahogany wooden sandals.

"Ropashna, I feel so much pressure," I say as soon as the Bullet zips away.

We walk along the dimly lit street, both of us checking our tech buttons to makes sure our parents haven't messaged.

"Sunare and Contra parents, huh?" I halfheartedly joke.

"Deslin, why did you tell me to meet you? You can't even put in effort to make a proper joke," she says.

Her straightforwardness used to be cute, but now it's just bothersome. I actually don't know why I called. It's better if we just keep working separately until whenever Ovatus strikes.

"Mm. I don't seem to do anything right, but I thought you had forgiven me," I mumble.

"What do you want me to say? Why would I be understanding when all you've done is continue to just lead me on? I hadn't properly worked through everything when you asked me to forgive you," she admits.

"Ropashna, I just need to talk. Please," I actually beg this time.

Her smooth face covers my peripheral vision, but I can't verify if her big brown eyes display remorse.

"What's up?" Ropashna finally says.

A few Bullets and herds of droids speed past, and the chilly wind increases its harshness.

"My parents want me to do something and I thought I wanted one thing, but maybe I want what they want. I don't know."

I reach for Ropashna's hand, desperate for some kind of connection, but she coldly bats me away.

"I know. It's hard for you. You can't live like this forever. You can't live for their approval all of the time," she flatly says.

Huh. She thinks I'm talking about The Traction Project.

"I'm not. I just need to do this. I've worked too hard to come this far. I have to keep pushing," I try to reassure myself.

"Deslin, you are capable. It is clear that you have spent your life growing up working on how hard you work, but just think about everything else. Seriously, how can you be so smart, so intelligent, yet lack such empathy skills? You lack this innate maturity that comes from exploring the world, not always studying, and working on your experiments all the time. There is so much more to life than just being the perfect one in the room, Deslin. You know this," Ropashna emotionlessly says right before jumping back into a Bullet gliding along the street like smooth ice.

She leaves before I have a chance to gather my thoughts and provide a response to reel her back in, but I know there's no use in even pretending like we want the same things anymore. I've made my choice and she's made hers.

CHAPTER 13

MAGAZINE MISHAPS: ROPASHNA

———

Today is the day I have to tell Ovatus how we're going to assassinate Influencer Anastasia. I still don't know if it's going to work, but at this point, it would be stupid to give up. Influencer Jeenz won't respond to me and I don't even know what's going on with Deslin.

Tucking a stray hair back into my secure and glossy ponytail and pulling down my tight light grey and florescent yellow, plaid-patterned pencil skirt, I click my sheeny red heels and walk to Influencer Brecky's office with one of the printed issues of the finished Mirror Mania Magazine. As I approach the office, I notice that her transparency setting is switched on, but she doesn't seem to notice. Scanning one of the smokey pink glass exterior walls, I peek at my doting reflection. *Still lookin' thick as hell, but gotta reduce that pooch, girl.*

Shooing away my semi-negative thoughts, I sink through Influencer Brecky's door and paste a distracting smile on my face.

"We did it! We finished. It's ready, it's here. It's Mirror Mania Magazine: Spring Issue!" I exclaim.

Influencer Brecky startlingly jumps, adjusts her nerdy thick frames, and gently caresses the glossy cover. Admiring Zasha's graphic design skills in constructing a modern-day Roman-sculptured god to pages of advertisements for booty boosting bourbon shots and perfect midpoint weight maintenance coaching, her eyes twinkle with excitement.

"Stunning. This is great! I'm glad all of the hard, um, work has paid off. We have to, um, distribute these now! Uh...Send out a crew to distribute throughout the building and we'll, um, work on sending out digital and print copies to the rest of the city," Influencer Brecky remarks.

"Sounds good. Also, I wanted to ask you something a bit personal, Brecky," I test, but sense her nervousness through her fidgeting and adjusting her already perfectly placed glasses.

"Hmm, what is it?" She peeps.

"Well, I know Influencer Anastasia comes in here quite a bit, but I also know she can be really rude to you, and I just wanted to ask why you put up with that?" I let out, tilting my head to display my genuine curiosity for an answer.

"Look, I'm an Influencer here, but I'm not that respected. I'm definitely not the prettiest or have the most proportional body, but at least I'm here. I'd rather be here than all those other people who can't even get into a convenience store because they can't take care of themselves properly," she says with an elongated heave at the end. She sounds guilty for speaking her truth.

She just seems like she needs support from people that feel guilty for being privileged.

"I see. The thing is though, 'those people' are people too. They deserve to go into a convenience store, you know? They deserve to wear clothes that make them feel good, regardless if they're under their low point or over their high point. MM Influencers are the ones who made these guidelines, but who's to say that they're even correct? Why can't people just judge themselves for what their own 'right' size is?" I feel myself burning inside, a little guilty that I'm not being secretive about my intentions.

Influencer Brecky's quiet, but she's thinking. Her pupils dilate, but then soften, and dilate again, trying to reason why I've barged in here with such a passionate attitude. I just want to convince her. I just want to show her that she doesn't have to live this way, like a damn robot. She just doesn't want to do the work; she doesn't want to be uncomfortable.

"Ropashna, I know you're not exactly...at your um, midpoint and that you were brought here under...*ahem* 'special circumstances.' However, I hope you know that it is, um, a privilege for you to be here," Brecky affirms. Her tech button beeps, and I realize that she's not worth the effort to convince.

Influencer Brecky just seems lost and willing to go with whoever is in power; she seems like she couldn't care less about being an Influencer at Mirror Mania.

As soon as I slip back outside, her office transforms into mirror covers again. The rest of the Communications and Analytics Department is dark because everyone went home as soon as the first page of the magazine was printed.

Heading to Ovatus, I already start feeling queasy and stressed with knowing I'm about to speak in front of everyone. I don't even know if Deslin is going to be there, but it doesn't matter. There's so much to be said, but it's just better if it's all left unsaid.

"How's everything going?" A platinum blonde head crosses my view before entering the mirror corridor.

"Influencer Jeenz....how's hideout? I'm talking to Ovatus right now. I have an entire plan on The Traction Project. We will be carrying it out very soon and I hope that you-" I immediately pour out my plans to Influencer Jeenz.

Her blank expression pauses my lips.

"Good. You're focused. That's all. It's unsafe for me here. Goodbye," she says without any kind of feedback.

What the hell? How can she put me in charge of all this and then just disappear? Whatever, I don't need her. I don't need anyone.

Finally reaching Ovatus, it's a lot more crowded than the last meeting. Even more people have joined: other interns, some older retired Influencers, young families. Zasha and Jrelito gallop over to me.

"You're gonna do amazing. Whatever the plan is, it's gonna be amazing!" Zasha repeats, embracing me into a comforting hug.

I smile at the floating platform I'm about to have to go on and see the immensely full room.

"Deslin ain't here, but it's gooch. You got this!" Jrelito attempts to do some kind of quirky handshake.

The room's chatter lightens, as I elegantly float up to the top of the room.

"Everyone, thank you for coming here today! I appreciate your support and confidence in me," I begin.

Light clapping and cheering commence. A few people tap their feet out of impatience.

"Now, I know we all need to figure out the exact steps to assassinate Influencer Anastasia. It'll be pretty simple. Our first protest will be in the Beauty Bio Space two days from now, destroying useless instruments and disgusting serums that have killed our fellow brothers and sisters," I go on.

Zasha and Jrelito whistle. Shojan smiles and jumps. Their approval eases my nerves.

"Our second protest will be right outside the entrance of Mirror Mania. The hope is that the rest of Speculo will join and the Influencers will not have a choice except to listen to us," I continue.

"That's great, but what about the biggest thing? The freaking assassination!" a loud, annoying intern shouts from below.

The rest of Ovatus cheers in approval, awaiting my response. My hands start trembling again.

"I'm getting to it! While protesting, we'll need a Beauty Bio Space intern because they know all the formulas, and Influencer Anastasia always loves to experiment with prototype injections. Jrelito, I will need you to develop a poisonous injection, while Zasha will carry out the rest. As the building will be empty from our distracting protest, Zasha will go to the Body Imaging Centre and take out Influencer Anastasia," I say all at once, clasping my hands to wait for any disapproval.

"Hell yeah! Let's do it!" Jrelito eagerly shouts back. Zasha sticks up her chipped manicure thumb in approval.

"Ropashna! Ropashna! Ovatus!" The whole room incessantly chants.

Everything feels complete. I feel light and on top of the world. Nothing is stopping me; nothing is stopping us.

Feeling a buzzing sensation, my tech button beeps from a Facegram notification from *Deslin*. What would he have to say? He wasn't even here for the meeting at Ovatus to hear about the next steps for the Traction Project.

"Motivation Room. Now," he messages.

"Can you be any more polite?" I half joke.

"Listen, I don't have time to joke right now. Just get here fast."

A pair of hazel eyes paints my vision as I swing out from the mirror corridor into the Motivation Room.

"You didn't think I would let you go so fast, now did you, Ropashna?" Deslin greets me.

"What do you want?" I say outright.

"I'm sorry about everything. I've just been so occupied because Influencer Jeenz has been demanding a lot more from me lately. Do you think you can forgive me? Can we be friends?" He tilts his head and steps closer to me.

My senses are fighting against the addicting smell of pine and what seems to be organic aloe vera scented hair gel. Still hard in my voice, my body speaks with limpness, permitting Deslin to wrap himself around me. I notice there's something different about his touch this time, though. It's not as thoughtful. He seems like he's lazily touching me just for the sake of touching.

"Is that a yes?" he gently whispers in my ear.

Maybe, if I just give him one more chance, maybe if I just wait and be patient, he will finally come around.

But I don't care. I don't care if we can't be friends and there's hostility. I don't care if people look at us badly or look at me badly. I don't care if he doesn't want to help me.

"No," I say as a I forcefully pull away.

I slink into the mirror corridor alone, leaving him with his lazy, veiny hands dwindling by his side.

CHAPTER 14

TWO SIDES: DESLIN

———

No longer being part of Ovatus feels different, but it feels more in line with who I am, or who I've become.

Influencer Jeenz dramatically sways her head to the unopened messages in her digital inbox on the glass projector of her office. We've been spending so much time together and it's weird to see her be girly or to just have some kind of range of emotions in general.

"Ovatus is getting bigger. What are we gonna do? We're still not ready to wipe out all the extreme low pointers and extreme high pointers," I say.

Jeenz glides over to me, bopping me on the nose. "Aaand you are correct! My secret little partner!" she uncharacteristically squeals.

Nothing seems to make sense anymore.

"Essentially, it's just going to be Influencers vs. Ovatus. We need some time to develop injections and organize each person registered as too below their low point weight or too above their high point weight. Based on Ropashna's information, they still want to attempt to assassinate Influencer Anastasia, so I am proposing we give them a week to prove themselves," she says, returning back to her monotone state.

"How do we do that?" I ask.

"Speak the truth. The rest of the Influencers, including you as the Head Assistant of Mirror Mania, and myself will just say that The Traction Project was a ploy. We will lie, saying if they want a chance to stay relevant in Speculo City, they have a week. This buys us time and them false hope," Jeenz states with not an inkling of sympathy.

Wow, I don't know if I want to just kill them all, but I guess with great power comes great sacrifice.

"Right. Do you actually believe in allowing them to prove themselves?" I question, already knowing the answer.

"Never. If they were worthy to do that, then they wouldn't be so low or so high in weight to begin with," Jeenz predictably answers.

From outside, there's muffled yelling and screaming. I see Influencer Anastasia and a bunch of Ovatus members. Of course, Ropashna's at the head.

"WE DEMAND CHANGE. NOW. WE ARE MORE THAN NUMBERS. WE ARE MORE THAN OUR WEIGHT," they seem to be yelling.

Anastasia frantically looks around, not knowing where to begin in order to calm such an emotional crowd. Jrelito empties tester bottles of *lose ten pounds in three days* diet weight loss pills, fat absorbing clamps, and protein injectors, while tearing down body weight requirement posters. Zasha keeps screaming and slashing anything in her way, throwing the latest issue of Mirror Mania Magazine on walls and floors. The rest of the members continue smashing all the other products I've been working so hard on; they must have already conquered most of the building already if they made it to the Beauty bio space.

I slowly inch forward, but a dry hand yanks my arms back into the dark hidden supply closet. Her raspy moans smoothly transcend into my ears, deep down inside the depths of my warm body.

"Desl...Deslin..." Jeenz gasps. Our fluttering eyes keep us in a trance away from all of the commotion and locked in our own passion. I only open mine to paint her neck by sinking my pearly whites into her delicious pillowy skin. She only opens hers to pull me in closer with her petite calves grasping around my toned abs.

"God, Jeenz. You're so fucking sexy..." I let out. Suddenly, this whole scenario feels too familiar; images of a beautiful brown eyed beauty pops in my head.

The first time I saw her at Intern Orientation. She was so different, so inspiring. What happened to me? What happened to us? But then, I remember she's not here. She's not on my side. She doesn't want to support me. Jrelito is acting like a savage and so is she. I don't have room for that in my life.

The clashing and screaming outside disintegrates. My veiny hands twirl around Jeenz's locks, while her tender lips pull on mine, forcing myself to forget about the girl I really want. Jeenz looks up at me with a sort of innocence that I never knew she even possessed, an innocence that made me feel wanted, *needed.* We're standing still now, no longer lost together, thinking our own thoughts.

She finally speaks, "Deslin, it's time to take over for sure. We have to create a society free from this notion of moderation and intuition and personal choice. We have to be the ones in control, to tell them that *restriction* is the leader of freedom."

I close my eyes hard, digging for a sense of concentration, but I feel depleted. I grab her again.

"Not now, Jeenz. Not now..." I whisper, trying to find that space where it was just the two of us again.

She doesn't resist me and connects herself to my full, juicy lips. But then, the lights turn on as fast as my realization that reality needs to be dealt with. There are light footsteps. I hear two sources of heavy breathing, one that sounds sexy, but the other sounds like preconceived anger and instant disappointment.

"Same place. Different girl, huh?" the other source of breathing shakes.

Surprisingly, I don't see the rest of Ovatus circled behind Ropashna. They're too occupied acting like ugly botdogs way too past their highest point and lowest point weights. I immediately pull away from Influencer Jeenz. Ropashna looks at me with confusion for a split second, but then immediately adjusts her hair, squashing any ounce of displayed vulnerability and empathy.

The sparkle from her brown eyes are replaced with extreme dullness. I can't speak.

"You could have just told me. You could have just said that you weren't ready, that you weren't fully ready to commit. You could have told me that I wasn't the girl you wanted. You could have just broken up with me first and then did whatever the hell you wanted..." The more she talks, the more she can't gather her thoughts. She's across the room, the lights are dim, but still bright enough for me to see faint lines on her face from her tear stains.

"I think I'm just...I'm just going to excuse myself," Influencer Jeenz awkwardly says, slowly dragging her body to the mirror doors.

"No! No. *You* don't get to leave. *You* betrayed me, too. I thought you believed in me. I thought you saw something in me, but I guess I was just a joke. I guess I'm too big or too much for you, so you went with Deslin because he's gorgeous and perfect, right? What happened to women supporting women? Oh, it's because you don't really *know* me, right? Well, Jeenz. You never even made the effort. You were too horny, too greedy, I don't fucking know," Ropashna furiously goes off.

Jeenz hardens, taking the form of who she regularly portrays herself to be. "Listen, you were just part of the ultimate plan. Deslin knows what he's doing. Did you really think I would need assistance from the likes of *you*? You have Ovatus, so if you really think you can beat me or Mirror Mania or whatever the hell you want to do, then by all means, try. You have nothing to lose, except, I mean, probably 20 pounds."

"I knew you didn't ever like me," Ropashna says, her voice shaking in exasperation.

"Well... do you deserve to be liked? Look at you. I just wanted to keep you and your kind in your righteous places. I needed to contain your desire to fight back and destroy this beautiful system I have continued to preserve for ages!" Jeenz actually raises her voice.

"How old *are* you?" Ropashna asks, widening her eyes in both disgust and terror. "No, you know what? It doesn't matter. Past your plastic surgery, chemical creams, and calorie-deficit-obsessed brain, I really did admire you. From woman to woman," Ropashna finds solace in her own answer.

"Well! Come at me then. See if you can really change a system. See if you can reverse systemic societal brainwashing! Ha!" Influencer Jeenz sneers, flipping her disheveled hair.

In shock, I still don't say anything. I want to sink inside these macro bottles. I feel lost, but I don't even know how to say how I feel anymore, especially to Ropashna.

"You really have nothing to say? You really have *nothing*?" Her eyes are red yet pleading me to hold her. She's spitting but wants my attention at the same time. "I gave you everything.

I trusted you! Don't you feel guilty at all? I was falling in love! Was I just not.... enough? My ass wasn't fat enough? My waist wasn't tight enough? I wanted to just grow with you, Deslin. That's all I ever wanted," Ropashna desperately cries.

Confused with my numbness, I question if I'm feeling too much or not feeling enough.

With calculation, I formulate the words, "Ropashna. I want to be at the top. This power, at least I can do something with it. What can I do at the bottom—destroy things and shout at people?" I cut her short.

I don't want to prolong her pain.

"I was so good to you, and you'll regret this! I was the best. What if I find someone else? You'll regret this," she gasps, while her mind is still underwater, knowing she's drowning.

"That's my burden. That's on me to deal with if you find someone else. Maybe, one day I will regret it, but I know this is the right decision in this moment," I say with certainty.

And it is. She's stunning, beautiful, everything I've ever wanted, but it doesn't feel right. I don't have my priorities straight. I don't feel like I've even accomplished much to be that worthy of her. We were never actually together and maybe I never technically cheated on her, but she at least deserves some kind of explanation.

I look at her, nodding with comfort, letting her swim alone to a destination that I don't even know where it will be. Looking back at the supply closet, guilt serenades my eyes. The flash of kissing Ropashna in the Motivation Room blinds me for a second, but I quickly snap back to reality.

Back at my desk, Jrelito's poppy red hair bobs with pondering and answering at the same time.

"Didn't I just see you destroying everything?" I ask incredulously.

Glancing over Jrelito's bony shoulder, I notice the rough finger-touched sketches and inky scratch notes on his mirror screen. Even Jrelito will end up knowing that I'm no longer with Ovatus.

"They are just new products to replace the old stuff we have in Mirror Mania and the ones we sell to the rest of Speculo. I've been working on better posters for what is truly 'healthy,' organic berry powder vitamins, and finding more ways to measure ourselves other than a number on the scale," he blabbers about projects I thought I once would be doing by his side.

I put my hand on his shoulder. "Jrelito, It's been nice—I.."

"Stop. Do not touch him. Do not touch. Anyone. Get out of here," Ropashna's fiery eyes dart over toward me.

The rest of Ovatus stands behind her, mimicking her aggressive stance.

"Ropashna! What you sayinnn, it's Deslin! You literally been getting dicked down by this mans!" Jrelito jokes.

I roll my eyes. Ropashna doesn't flinch at all.

"How are you going to contradict yourself? How are you going to preach about how all those kids made fun of you, but now you're aiming to be just as shitty as them?" Zasha spits at me, standing behind Ropashna's scowl.

Ovatus roars. Jeenz is nowhere to be found. Anastasia backs herself into a corner, too afraid to be near people that are way beyond or below their low and high points, as if they'll be the ones to influence her instead. Brecky just stands in the middle, waiting for someone to win, so she can continue existing.

"Aha! That's exactly how we do it!" Jrelito scrambles his hands around and looks around the room, as if Ropashna isn't outing me for my betrayal in front of everyone. The crowd still roars.

Jrelito's red hair bounces around, while standing up from his seat. He nonchalantly looks at me and nods his head.

"It's aight, bro. I been knowing. I been knew since yo old man's party. I understand. I know you and you just gotta do what you gotta do," he says with calmness.

What happens when you've been on a path for so long that you forget why you were on it? What happens when you think you know what you've always wanted, but then it doesn't seem to be so simple anymore?

I snap out of it and nod my head toward Jrelito. Just like that, we understand one another.

"I promise I won't kill ya, but I don't know about your little Jeenz ho," he nudges my rib. All of a sudden, Jrelito seems smarter. He seems bigger, stronger.

"She's not my ho... but I guess we both gotta do what we both gotta do, right?" I purse my lips.

"I wish you were on the right side. We're all good. We just want to live life, a day even, without thinking about food all the time, without thinking about how that scale determines every single part of our self-worth," Jrelito says.

"I know, but then what? How does Speculo survive? This whole economy is literally built upon people believing they're not good enough. How can you *free* everyone then, huh?" I try to convince him.

"You just... of all people, I thought you would understand. I admire your motivation, your drive for your parent's approval, but seriously. Really, ask yourself, if you're on the right side, dude. Ask yourself if what you want out of life is to make millions by sacrificing people just because of the way they look," Jrelito says, surprising me again as to how eloquent he has the potential to sound.

"I should go," I say to cut the conversation short, leaving out as much emotion as possible.

"Hm. It's always the ones who don't show it that hurt the most," I overhear Zasha saying to Jrelito. They chuckle, but don't smile.

I stand at the front of the Beauty Bio Space, calling Jeenz on my tech button, projecting her flawless face widely on a clear, available wall. The protestors in Ovatus frantically look up and pause from clashing around everything.

"I'm sure you're all wondering why I decided to quit the Traction Project. Well, the truth is, I was never even in it. I want you all to know that it is inherently challenging to escape a profitable system like Mirror Mania. Influencers run everything. We are the law. We are the healthcare system. We are the government. We control Facegram," Jeenz keeps listing on and on.

"Blah blah blah, Jeenz. You keep repeating the same shit. We've literally physically destroyed more than half of this place already. We will get our way. The public already knows about the sacrifices and how their caloric needs are all based off of some unattainable goal to be a random, unsustainable number. How are the two of you going to stop a whole city?" Ropashna retorts.

"Yeah! The days of wanting to be an influencer are long gone. People want to pursue other goals now. They want to own their own businesses, they want to be artists, they want to have a life purpose other than achieving some unrealistic standard," Zasha adds on, sounding like a necessary sidekick.

I stand in silence. What they're saying is convincing and it all makes sense, but the glory of the traditional sense of power is all too consuming: a feeling of control that I've never truly experienced, or at least have longed to experience. I just don't want to give it up yet.

"Honestly, whatever you guys say makes sense, but it's just not going to happen! I'll tell you what. You guys surprise me. Surprise me and convince me to simply dismantle Mirror Mania, leaving it to be a historical statue. You have one week to impress me! Until then, you are all banned from here. It's Ovatus versus Influencers," she mocks Ovatus, as beeping sounds of tech buttons serenade the room with a melody of fear and anxiety.

"I hope you guys learn that it's just easier this way. Continuing to go on with this system allows people to buy into a dream that only the 1 percent can achieve. Why do you guys want to do all this hard work to be in tune with yourselves or to have some higher purpose other than looking as perfect as possible?" I support Jeenz, sounding like a necessary sidekick.

"Because it's not who we are anymore. It's not what we live for anymore. Food is the fuel, not something we worship. We want full lives; we don't want to be bound by the numbers. How many times do I have to tell you? Or is this what happens when you don't know yourself? You're confused all the time. That's why you're with Jeenz. She's like a sexy mom to you, huh?" Ropashna dryly says with a voice coated in sarcastic pity.

I shrug, pretending like I'm not doubting myself on where I stand. *I didn't mean to hurt you,* I think to myself.

"Do you really think you're going to end up assassinating Anastasia? Do you even have it in you?" I retort back instead.

"Especially after what you did to me, I guess you and your little mommy friend will have to wait and see," Ropashna pouts, pushing herself back into the crowd of delusional losers.

CHAPTER 15

TWO SIDES: SHATTERED

———

Since Jeenz has given us a week to fight for our lives, Ovatus has been working nonstop. We've been telling more people, making more flyers, protesting, and doing the low work, but tomorrow is our last day before the Influencers completely take over Mirror Mania and Speculo City for good.

"Ropa! We want to help you in any way possible," Dad says.

"Yeah, dude. I joined Ovatus because I believe in the cause. Mirror Mania is so traditional, and Speculo City's future doesn't involve constant monitoring or judging ourselves by unrealistic standards. Seriously? When did we start to look at Facegram to tell us how to live our lives?" Shojan ponders to the family.

"For a while, now. We decided that religion and doctors and universities and even more longstanding institutions were useless; we turned to Facegram because we thought it would be more liberating," Mom explains.

"It's interesting that when you have so much freedom, you feel trapped because you don't know how to make choices. You have so many options that you don't know which is the best one," Dad says in agreement with Mom.

I'm quiet because I find it interesting that it has taken so much action from Ovatus to finally wake up the city. Mirror

Mania has done a marvelous job at systemic brainwashing, but it still amazes me that people haven't realized how atrocious this way of living is on their own.

"Ropashna, we are so very proud of you," Mom says. Dad nods his head. He doesn't really say things like that, but I can tell from his actions that is what he's trying to communicate.

"I just don't know what to do with all this stress of trying to convince Jeenz and all the people at their perfect mid-point weights in general. Of course, they don't want things to change," I say, feeling a bit defeated.

Mom rubs her soft, pillowy hands on my back.

"Oh, Ropa... I know it's hard, but you will think of something. Why aren't you with Ovatus right now?" Mom asks.

"Yeah! We can head over to meet up with everyone now!" Shojan wishfully encourages.

I nod my head, feeling too numb from processing all of the things with Deslin and Jeenz. I still feel too angry to even understand my own feelings about it.

"They all just keep asking me for instructions, as if I'm supposed to know what to do more than what we've discussed with protesting in front of Mirror Mania."

"I hate to stress you out more, but you don't really have much time. You don't have to be alone in coming up with something. We can all help you. That's why Ovatus exists," Shojan says with calming directness.

"We're always a team. I'm just glad you're old enough to realize that now, Ropa," Shojan continues on with a warm smile.

"By the way, how are you doing with the whole...you know," Shojan leads on.

Suddenly, my nose feels clogged and my teeth grit against each other.

"What? Deslin? Oh. I don't even know anymore. I just seem to attract people that just refuse to open themselves up, you know. It's frustrating. I feel like a damn orange that everyone is attracted to because I'm bright and sweet with a layer that requires barely an effort to peel off," I say with a sigh of frustration.

"Yeah, I know. We're a super emotional and caring family that doesn't like to hide anything from each other. I think you already know the reason why you and Deslin didn't work wasn't really because of you, Ropa. It was because of him and his own fears to confront himself," Shojan explains.

I hear what he's saying, but I struggle to listen to his words. It makes sense, but I just don't want to accept it all yet.

"But hey, enough of that. You'll probably see him today, and I just wanted to make sure that you're prepared for that. Don't let him distract you from what's important. He's not on your team, no matter what he says. Remember that," Shojan sternly says, but with brotherly affection.

We meet up with everyone at Ovatus not to discuss our plans, but to feel like we're all still in this together.

"Listen up! The poisonous injection has been developed!" Jrelito goes around blurting.

"And I am super ready to inject!" Zasha enthusiastically bursts with her bubbly attitude.

I smile with Shojan, feeling supported and reassured that we have a chance after all. I'm not even thinking about Deslin and his stupid face anymore.

"Hello everyone! I'm glad that we are all still motivated and ready to go. There aren't any new plans. We are still protesting in front of Mirror Mania today and the assassination plan will continue to be carried out," I yell out, too lazy to stand on the floating platform.

The room acknowledges me with cheers and hoots. We all hike back outside to take in the drowsy, dreary Noveria sky. Circling back to the main entrance of Mirror Mania, a mysterious charcoal gate blocks the view, along with a group of fancily dressed Influencers with Jeenz and Deslin at the front. I hate them. I hate them even more than Anastasia and my shitty childhood checkups with her.

"Hey, you gonna be okay? Jrelito and I are about to sneak back in through the hidden way to Ovatus soon," Zasha leans her soft head on my weirdly aching shoulder.

Everything aches when I feel disappointed.

"Yeah, go on ahead. We have to do this. This is why we came to Mirror Mania in the first place," I say.

Was it really why we came?

Moving forward, I lead the rest of Ovatus to the gate. I don't stop, pushing myself over the poles.

"Are you deaf?! I already told you that you aren't allowed in here anymore, you fat, ugly bitch! You're 30 pounds over your maximum weight limit, so leave already!" a coarse, harsh voice bleeds into my ears.

I'm the reason that the line to Mirror Mania is backed up, but I don't care. My thick thighs hinge themselves over the greased charcoal gate, pleading to be let in. Tears fill my eyes and my throat clenches.

"Someone take this fatty away please!" Jeenz yells right in my face and nonchalantly shoos me away with her hand, as if we had no type of relationship.

I start screaming, yelling, and cursing, trying to get one of the Influencers to see I'm on the right side of things. Am I on the right side of things?

Suddenly, my performance is interrupted, and *he* sprints toward me. He's wearing his tight black skinsuit with an embroidered *MM* near his collarbone and leather combat boots. I can't stand my ground any longer, my hair falls in front of my face as I slump into his strong, moon-tattooed, veiny arms: a place that once felt so comforting.

"What are you doing?" I manage to let out.

"You wanted to get over the gate, so here you fucking go," he whispers to me.

Regaining my consciousness, I notice the Influencers and Jeenz run toward the rest of Ovatus. Jrelito and Zasha are nowhere to be found, but I trust them. Everyone crowds the streets and steps in a trance of hair pulling, name calling, throwing powdery bits of Cheezbits, clashing around fat zap tools, throwing off waist cinchers. Everyone looks the same. It's all violence that brings us closer, yet further apart.

"Why couldn't you guys just forfeit? It would have been so much easier. Ovatus doesn't have the willpower. Assassinating Anastasia will do *nothing*," Deslin continues speaking to me as I lay over his shoulder.

"You don't know what it's like to be bullied for *who you are*. It's like the whole world tells you, 'You there! You are not allowed to be Deslin. No. That's not good enough. You are not allowed to be you.' Have you ever felt that? I'm reminded of that so much from myself, from my parents, that I have so much motivation to show them that I am allowed to be Deslin," he infuriatingly shouts, heaving from his own anger.

I quickly jump off of him ready to defend myself.

"Why do you talk as if I haven't been through shit, too? Just because I don't make it my life goal to avenge those that wronged me when I could barely think for myself doesn't mean I haven't been through things. You like to single yourself out with your experiences because you know that they're not even that special, but you love to drown in your pain because it makes you feel unique," I fire back at him.

He's the one who hurt *me*. He's the one who should feel bad. He's the one that's wrong. Screaming in the crowd continues. My head starts pounding

"I'm not out here thinking that I'm some special, 'nobody will ever understand me' sort of way, but what I said is true. You haven't been through anything that I've had to go through. Do you know what it's like when you're your own biggest bully? When I would force myself to eat less, to look a certain way, and think that I still wasn't good enough? I thought that I was predestined to live my life according to the number on the scale, not by how I feel or what my body was telling me," my mouth unleashes, as if I can't control what's coming out of it.

I can't stop my words from shooting at him. I can't stop even though I know just one shot would be enough to kill him.

"You've talked about that. It's just different when someone affirms all of that for you, Ropashna. That's what I mean. It's even worse when you think that, and some random white skinny kid comes along and repeats those same lines of death in your head," Deslin lets out a heavy sigh.

It's all too much. I can't hold on to principles just for the sake of holding on because it feels fake. I don't know if Jrelito and Zasha carried through the plan, but I hope they know better than me at this point because Ovatus doesn't kill. Ovatus was never meant to kill. We just believed that because Jeenz manipulated our desperateness for equality.

"You hurt me, Deslin. You hurt me so *freaking* bad," I finally admit the raw truth to him, looking into his tired hazel eyes.

"I know, Ropashna. I'm sorry. I really am. For me, there was nothing really about you that held me back. It was about the fear I had. It was about being scared about trusting some-one and not knowing where it was going to go. It was about being scared of myself and who I would become if I fully invested in something," Deslin tenderly responds.

Without warning, my head stops pounding. The air seems a bit clearer, and the noise no longer becomes distracting.

"I know. It's okay. We don't have to do this. What are we doing? We're all fighting for the same thing. We all just want to live the way we want to," I say to him and myself.

Deslin just nods, trying to soak in the same realization. Ovatus and the Influencers can work together. We don't have to kill each other like this. We don't have to be on opposite sides trying to destroy each other, trying to be each other. Running toward the crowd, I immediately call over a droid to lift me up, so everyone can see me.

"Stop! Everyone, stop! Look at yourselves. Whether you're an Influencer or you're part of Ovatus, you most likely didn't join to do all this," I say, gesturing to the mess of fatty snacks and pieces of fake hair all over the dirty, blood-spotted ground.

Anastasia's silver-striped colored contacts enter my view. A sense of relief washes over me, as Zasha and Jrelito wave at me with knowing smiles that they didn't go through with the assassination.

"This is Mirror Mania. We look at ourselves in the mir-rors, but we all have the choice to see how we view ourselves. Influencers, I know you guys are sick of these unrealistic standards too. Mirror Mania physically doesn't have to change! Our *mindsets* do. We can use the mirror to embrace our natural bodies. We can use the scale to maintain our health. It's not about destroying, it's about finding balance. It's about finding moderation," I preach on with all my might and courage.

At first, it's completely quiet, except for the beeping of droids and kids giggling at the nearby Mirror Maze.

"Yeah! She's right!" Brecky, of all people, cheers out.

"Yeah! Let's go Ropashna! Moderation! We can all do this together!" Shojan, Jrelito, and Zasha all say in unison.

I smile and my heart starts beating faster. The whole crowd starts cheering, until I see Jeenz's blank face.

"Well, it would limit our monopoly of power. However, I do see the benefit in which Mirror Mania could be more profitable if it appealed to all types of demographics," Jeenz surprisingly reasons out.

The other Influencers start smiling too, throwing and ripping off their tight shapewear to the ground, exposing rolls and cellulite printed stomachs.

"It's about working together, and we can. It's about love and health. It's okay to want to look good, but it's also okay if you're not at a certain weight. Mirror Mania doesn't have to be feared. It can be a place of empowerment now," I keep preaching.

Jeenz nods her head in approval, followed by Anastasia and Deslin, and the rest of the Influencers. After I trickle down from the droid's grasp, the rest of Ovatus cheers, hugging me and squeezing me out of appreciation. My cheeks feel warm and I can't stop smiling. This wasn't what I had planned; this isn't what any of us had planned.

"I can't thank you guys enough for not going through with the assassination," I plead to Zasha and Jrelito, tightly embracing them.

I've never felt so close to people in such a short amount of time.

"We just knew that it wasn't the goal for Ovatus and for you. We knew that assassinating a major influencer would just cause even more tension and less justice," Zasha says.

"Yup! What she said!" Jrelito seconds.

The crowd cheers and everyone hugs. A few people even start kissing and holding each other as if they were hiding their own secret relationships.

"You did it, Ropashna. You broke the cycle," Deslin quietly says behind me.

"It was so simple, but so hard to execute," I sit down on the steps of the Mirror Mania entrance.

"That's usually how letting go works," he chuckles.

Deslin and I don't say anything else because we just got out of one cycle and there's no point in starting another one. Forgiveness is the real reason why Mirror Mania, Ovatus, equality, compassion, and acceptance are all appealing to everyone in Speculo City. We aren't supposed to destroy Mirror Mania, we are just supposed to look at it differently. We're all free to be who we are—to look good and feel good in the ways we want.

The mirror doesn't choose how we see ourselves. We choose how we see ourselves in the mirror.

ABOUT THE AUTHOR

———

Ever since I had basic motor skills, writing became my passion. As I continued to be more involved in the arts world from such a young age, my creativity continued to fuel my craft.

As I grew up, I started trying other activities, and I'm someone who struggles when it comes to balance. I love to do it all, but it usually just leads to me doing nothing at all!

When I reached high school, I had stopped writing for leisure because I thought it was pointless and not "productive." I even ended up applying to twelve universities because I thought nursing was my calling!

When I reconnected with writing, I felt so much lighter and freer: the same feeling I had when I was just a little girl with less responsibility.

Always on the go and always striving to be better, writing provides me comfort, escape, novelty, and reflection. I love meeting new people and sharing their stories through words on a page.

Mirror Mania is my first—but definitely not last—book. I can't wait to keep impacting my local communities and creating for as long as I can. There's always room for improvement and growth.

As my high school senior quote was "I will change the world someday," I hope that with this book, with my words, I can achieve that goal one page at a time.

~Roveena Chand Jassal

ACKNOWLEDGEMENTS

—

I want to acknowledge New Degree Press and everyone who was very involved in my book journey.

A special thank you to the ones who saw potential in me before I saw it in myself and encouraged me when I needed it the most:

Mom and Dad, Justin, Mandela, Mr. Sanders, Disha, Keerthana, Apoorva, Serina, Pav, Suga, Dhanbir, Rish, Mrs. Fuhrer, Mr. Sanders, Eric Koester, Abdalla, and Dean Henderson.

Thank you to my expert editors and avid fans of my work:

New Degree Press, Mozelle, Melody, Her Campus Western, Ethan, Britt, Jumana, and Sarah.

I would also like to thank Aishwarya Raj, Natasha and Sunil Menezes, Sherylann and Nalesh Phillips, and Sabrina Hope for ordering two copies of Mirror Mania!

Lastly, a huge acknowledgement to Mrs. Ginny Gates who preordered five whole copies of Mirror Mania!

SUPPORTER ACKNOWLEDGMENTS

———

I'd like to acknowledge everyone who preordered my book for giving me the opportunity to publish Mirror Mania and believing in me as both a writer and young woman to pursue her dreams:

Abdalla Abdelhady	Ashley Li
Adithya Raghu	Azia To
Aishwarya Raj	Baani Khurana
Ajay Bhatia	Baljinder Jassal
Akshat Saxena	Bhaswati Laha
Amanda Dominguez	Brady Park
Anchal Sharma	Brittany Chang-Kit
Anisha Kapoor	Chantal Hermetz
Apoorva Saxena	Charlotte Afonso

Charis Lai

Chelsea Ho

Chiquíta Chatterjee

Chris and Windy Holder

Chukwuma Chukwueke

Courtney Reich

Daniel Roy

Danielle M. Sequeira

Denise and Greg Schaffer

Dhanbir Singh Thethi

Disha Natalia

Disha Rawal

Dwight Nelson

Eric Koester

Erin Matus

Ethan Shi

Eustace imafidon

Gabrielle Zuvic

Gavin and Tanya Soares

Grover Family

Harry and Gindi Jassal

Hark and Cynthia Jassal

Hellen Yun

Isaias Lopez

Jacob Sanders

Jania Hemnani

Jasmine Saluja

Jasvir Singh

Jeff Orchard

Jean-Paul M. and Boluwa Massina

John and Maria Fernandes

Jorge Guerreiro

Juan-Luis Suárez

Julia Campbell

Jumana Labib

Justin James

Justin Jassal

Keerthana Sharath

Keith Alvares

Kiara Ambersley

Leah Bessner

Lisa Henderson

Mandela Massina

Mandy Gill

Manmohan Kaur

Mara Porada

Marilyn and Jerry D'Souza

Mark Simon

Matthew McLean

Mayank Kesarkar

Michael Card

Michele and Prem Britto

Millie and Jack Dsouza

Mrs. Ginne Gates

Muhammad Aamir

Nafisa Husain

Navdeep Jassal

Neelesh and Nisha Shanbhag

Nilesh and Sherylann Phillips

Nula Dabreo

Olivia Collins

Parminder and Kamal Jassal

Paul and Sonia Jassal

Pavneet Kaur Singh

Prachi Patel

Prafulla and Tom Dsouza

Pranav Perepa

Precious Adekoya

Priya and Shastri

Rafael Montano

Rani Trivedi

Rishika Sekhar

Rishwanth Sunkara

Robbie and Katelynn

Romita Dayal

Ruchika and Joey Walia

Sabrina R. Hope

Sailaxmi Korada

Sandy Smeltzer

Sanjeev and Poonam Pandey

Sarah Wallace

Sarita and Santosh Pinto

Savinder K. Bhatia

Sebastian and Mandeep Serwa

Serina Chahal

Shalini and Melville D'Souza

Shefali Bhatt

Srijan Khare

Stefanie Tom

Suga Saravanan

Sunil and Natasha Menezes

Sunjay Ghai

Susan Fuhrer

Sydney Joao

Thomas Streeter

Tirath and Manjit Singh

Tricia Johnson

Vasudha Pandey

Victoria Wolff

Xzavier M. Stewart

Zahra Fatina

APPENDIX

───────

AUTHOR'S NOTE

"Statistics and Research on Eating Disorders." National Eating Disorder Association. Accessed on August 5, 2020. https://www.nationaleatingdisorders.org/statistics-research-eating-disorders

Westover, Sophia. "8 Body Positive and Inclusive Sustainable Fashion Brands." *Attire Media.* July 19, 2020. https://www.attiremedia.com/discover-all/8-body-positive-and-inclusive-sustainable-fashion-brands

CPSIA information can be obtained
at www.ICGtesting.com
Printed in the USA
FSHW021318121220

9 781636 766249